THE CROSSING

Breakfast was long behind them and the morning sun was getting hot when the call came back to "squeeze 'em down." The river crossing was coming up, and the point riders wanted the herd bunched together. The Wichita! . . .

When it came Bannon's turn, he removed his clothes quickly and stuffed them into a small cloth bag. . . . He swung up into the saddle and cantered back into position. His throat was tight. "Please don't let me foul up, Lord," he prayed.

All the trail stories of vicious river crossings where men and animals had died came bouncing into his young mind. Unexpected things of every sort could kill the best of trail hands: High, rushing water could knock a man silly; undercurrents could pull a horse down and keep it there; there might be quicksand where it didn't look like there was any; you could get slammed into by steers that went crazy in the water.

Only a fool wouldn't be worried.

DARK TRAIL TO DODGE

COTTON SMITH

LEISURE BOOKS NEW YORK CITY

To Sonya—
Who rides beside me
on the trail of life
and makes it good.

A LEISURE BOOK®

April 1999

Published by special arrangement with Walker Publishing Company.

Dorchester Publishing Co., Inc.
276 Fifth Avenue
New York, NY 10001

ISBN 0-8439-4510-9

The name "Leisure Books" and the stylized "L" with design are trademarks of Dorchester Publishing Co., Inc.

Printed in the United States of America.

DARK TRAIL
TO DODGE

CHAPTER 1

"CHECK OVER THAT ridge there, Ty. See that cow a-bawlin'? She's got a calf in trouble, I reckon. Yeah, over there."

Without hesitating, Tyrel Bannon followed the trail boss's command. Reining his sweaty black horse, he headed for the broken ridge twenty yards south of the trail herd. On a parallel knoll behind the ridge, a large-boned, longhorn cow stood, too agitated to go anywhere.

Dan Mitchell, the savvy trail boss with the everpresent chaw, spat a long brown stream of tobacco and kicked his horse into a lope. He didn't look back to see if Bannon did as asked: a compliment to a green hand. Behind them, the Triple C herd was a brown mass, waltzing slowly over a half mile of the Staked Plains of Texas.

The swale between the front ridge and the knoll could hide almost anything out here. The farm boy had learned this the hard way, as he had everything else on his first trail drive. On the second day, he had loped over similar ground only to find a range bull itching for trouble. His horse had bolted and tossed him unceremoniously in the leaving.

This time he eased his horse slowly up the rising. Near the top of the front ridge, he stood tall in the stirrups to peer over. The young cowboy saw the cow's problem and the trail boss was right, as usual. Her calf was trapped knee-deep in a triangular bog next to a small ford they'd just crossed. No way could the scrawny youngster get out, in spite of all its jerking and bawling. At least the bog didn't appear to be quicksand. Just heavy mud.

Stepping down from the saddle, he grabbed his rope

1

and threw a soft loop over the crying calf's head. He wasn't much of a roper. Yet. His late father had showed him how to plow and plant but not how to handle a lariat. A little girl could've hit this target though, he mumbled.

Standing at the bog's edge so he wouldn't get his old boots in the mud, Bannon began to pull. He was average-sized and slim-waisted, but hard farm work had made his arms and shoulders deceptively strong. The farm boy's long blond hair was quickly damp with sweat as the calf still did not budge. Streaks slid down his angular, sun-burned face, across his hawkish nose and the handful of freckles paraded there. He stopped, breathed deeply; his bright blue eyes studied the muddied animal.

"Come on, little fella," he coaxed, "that's no place for you. Your ma's all worried. Let's get outta there."

Again, he pulled with all of his strength. No movement. To make things worse, the calf even seemed to be straining against him. Bannon drew on the rope again. Harder this time.

"Come on, boy. Come on. Just one step. One little step. You can do it," the young man whispered, sweat beads popping out on his forehead. Maybe his gentle words would make the animal feel safe coming toward him.

Nothing. Absolutely nothing. Only a few feet away, the cow was drawing closer and bellowing louder. Her tongue lay long and pink toward the ground. Annoyed at her in-sistence, Bannon glanced over as if to assure her that he was doing the best he could. The cow wasn't impressed and kept up her demands.

There were only a handful of cows and calves in this herd of forty-one hundred beeves headed to Dodge City. It was made up of mostly four- and five-year-old longhorn steers and some three- and four-year-old she cattle with dry bags. This was one of the weaker pairs of mother and calf caught up in the roundup.

"Now look here. I've got better things to do than this," he told the perplexed calf, pointing at himself with his right thumb while holding the rope with his left fist, "I'm a flank rider . . . not a nursery boy. You get outta there!"

Bannon glanced around for a tree to provide more leverage. None were close enough to help. A huge, shaggy cottonwood was the nearest, over twenty feet away. Suddenly the young rascal jerked backward. Stumbling forward from the jolt, Ty caught his boots in the front edge of the deep muck and fell headlong into the black mess. For an instant, the young cowboy lay there, not sure what had happened. His face was splattered; his hat was off on its own adventure; his hands had disappeared into the sludgy mess, and his legs were swimming in it.

Slowly, he looked up. Innocent eyes stared down at him. He couldn't remember feeling so foolish. Except for the first day out when his green-broke brown horse threw him. At least this time no one saw him, he rationalized.

Working to find solid ground to stand on, slipping with every other step, he slowly freed himself from the bog. With his muddy hands still holding the now muddy rope, Bannon gave the calf a chewing out.

"I've got a good mind to leave you here. How would you like that? Why, the coyotes'd be around you quicker than your tail can switch!"

He stopped talking. It gave him the shivers to think of this little thing in such a fix. An idea crossed his mind: maybe he shouldn't look at the animal when pulling. Some horses didn't like to be stared at when led. That, he'd learned the hard way too.

Bannon turned his back and yanked with the rope over his shoulder. Something moved! He was sure of it and kept on pulling with everything he had. Along came the trail boss's dog to help. A three-legged cattle dog on the drive, Captain's barking perked some more energy into the calve's struggle to free himself. Finally, the calf stepped out of the bog, leaving Bannon coated with mud but grinning shyly at his achievement.

Satisfied, Captain went back with the herd. He was an ugly black cur, but the trail boss was proud of him. A right front leg had been lost five years earlier from a steer's kick, but it hadn't slowed him down. Mitchell was the only one he took orders from—or who could pet him without receiving a snarl.

Grinning at the calf shaking his body to remove the slick coating, the young cowboy gave it a slap on the rump. Not that it was needed. The little thing was eager to find his now quiet mother. Bannon rode behind the cow and calf, easing them along at a gentle lope until they came to the remuda, bringing up the rear.

Guiding the cow and her offspring around the horses, he heard the remuda's lanky wrangler, Randy Reilman, cursing loudly. The swearing was normal; rarely did a sentence come out of his mouth without a sprinkling of cuss words. Reilman was the "ketcher" in the morning selection of horses. Everyone went to him to rope their "mornin' hoss."

Bannon waved. "How you doin', Randy?"

Grumpily, Reilman returned the greeting, "Gawddamnsonvabitch, boy! Better'n you, I reckon. I would've left that goddamn calf if it'd be me. Nobody's gonna git me in that goddamn slop. No sir. Get up thar, hoss, you hell-for nuthin', crazy-eyed fool!" His rope-burned hands swung a lariat at a bay nipping at the brown horse running beside it.

In a few minutes, the young cowboy caught up with the drag riders and the back end of the herd. The cow and calf settled into a comfortable position in front of the slowest animals. Bannon really hoped that was the last he'd see of that pair for a while.

Today was only the second time he hadn't been at the drag himself. Mitchell had elevated him to a flank rider for this stretch of the drive. The hard-working farm boy was so proud of that recognition he nearly burst. Riding flank put the young cowboy at the back third of the herd; ahead in distance and responsibility were the swing riders and the two point riders.

He might not know anything about beeves, but hard work was no stranger. His mother had seen to that, especially since his father died of the fever two years back. And then his older brother, Samuel, was taken by the same illness. Bannon became the man of the house at sixteen.

Dodge City, Queen of the Cowtowns, was the drive's destination to fulfill a contract. It was the Triple C's first time to that market; previous drives had been to Ellsworth. But Dodge was much closer. The farmers had fenced off most of the other trailheads; they didn't want any part of Texas steers tromping over their crops.

There were fourteen drovers, plus a cook, a wrangler, a calf wagon driver, and the trail boss. Starting from the Triple C range near the Colorado River, they had already successfully crossed the Brazos, heading north. The river was low and didn't live up to the savage reputation Bannon's fellow riders had talked about around the campfire.

Roundup had been his first taste of cowboying. He hadn't been much help, he had conceded to himself. Mostly gawking at the smooth way the others worked. A black eye was his reward for trying to hold down a calf that didn't want to be branded.

Charlie Chance Carlson, owner of the Triple C and a friend of Bannon's late father, had hired him on, purely out of charity. He felt sorry for his friend's widow and knew the extra dollars her son would bring back would help. And it wouldn't look like a handout either: Abigail Bannon would have no part in accepting charity. Although

Dan Mitchell hadn't been too pleased to nursemaid a greenhorn on a tough drive, he had agreed to Carlson's quiet request.

"Whatcha been doin', boy? Takin' a mud bath?"

The sarcastic taunt cut through the dusty air of the drag. Henry Seals followed his yell with a sneer. A cigarette dangled from his lip as he watched the young rider advance, streaked with drying mud. Seals's blunt face was dominated by a thick nose, unruly eyebrows, and light gray eyes. They reminded Bannon of a wild animal's stare—on edge, wary. He was tall and muscular; his athletic movement and scarred knuckles bespoke of a natural fighter. He didn't like Bannon; his hate started on the drive's first day. Seals and somebody else had placed a large burr under Bannon's saddle blanket. The farm boy's half-broken paint horse got the bit in its mouth and took him for a spin, trying to rid itself of the sticking pain on its back. In the whirling and bucking, he banged into Seals and his horse, throwing both riders. Seals had been jeered as much as Bannon by the rest of the hands.

Seals's teasing was more than hazing a first-time trail hand. He was a mean, insolent man who took pleasure in making fun of others when they weren't around—or baiting a man to his face if Seals thought he wouldn't talk back. Like Tyrel Bannon. The farm boy had decided it wasn't his place to talk back. Not that jawing was much to his fancy anyway. Doing was a lot more important than talking, he figured.

The other drag riders joined in. "You been plowin' again, farm boy?" "Hey, let's call him Mudface!" "Don'tcha know you're supposed to get 'em out, not go swimmin' with 'em?" "That's a right nice shade o' brown you're wearin'. Goin' to a dance?" "Yeah, a mud dance!" "You oughta wear that same outfit into Dodge. Them gals like a muddy fella. Makes 'em warm an' soft." They laughed loudly at each other's jokes.

The slump-shouldered Irishman, Harry Clanahan, edged his horse next to the young rider, "Bannon, darlin', a fine Little Mary ye be makin', I'm a-thinkin'." Clanahan grinned his toothy smile as he said it.

Little Mary was the nickname they had given the driver of the calf wagon carrying the newborn calves that couldn't keep up otherwise. Some trail bosses would have killed the calves. Not Mitchell.

Seals cracked again, "I reckon the boy's done been eatin' cow pies! Wait a minute—that don't look like mud to me."

Turning red in the face, Bannon managed a thin smile.

The tall, square-jawed rider everyone called Wonson hollered out, "Thar's a great big mud hole a-comin' up, so's you kin git good n' black thar, boy."

Wonson was short for "one song," since that was all the cowboy ever sang to the cattle. It was a strange-sounding conglomeration of words that didn't rhyme. Sort of a cross between "In the Sweet By And By" and "Old Dan Tucker." Wonson didn't seem to mind being called that; his real name was Herman T. Carmen.

"Ya can still skedaddle back to your mommy, boy," Seals called out as Bannon rode away. "I'll bet you suck your thumb every night just thinkin' about her. Or maybe Daddy Mitchell tucks you in."

Kicking the black into a lope harder than it needed or deserved, the young rider left the drag and slid into his empty flank position. Everything in him was taut. His jaws were clenched hard. Here and now! He would take that bastard apart! No, no, that wasn't the way. He took a long deep breath, trying to let out the anger without boiling over.

He felt that if he couldn't take it, he should go home. Besides, even Seals had forgotten more about trail driving than Bannon knew so far—and Seals wasn't much of a drover at all. And no trail boss wanted his men fighting each other instead of watching beeves.

Back home, he would have taken Seals on or just hauled into all of them and let the fight take its course. But out here, he knew it wasn't the answer. Probably wasn't at home either, but it usually worked. The farm boy hadn't lost many fistfights.

Oh, there was the time Jared Simpson coldcocked him, but that didn't count, he reflected. Sucker punch, it was. Should've expected it, though. They were both sweet on the same little gal. She had a purely devilish smile and a figure to match. He got Simpson good the next time around. By then, though, she was sweet on some fellow clear over in the next county.

There wasn't anything personal in the other men's teasing. At least he didn't think so. The surly Seals simply thought he could bully the young rider. He figured silence was fear. Well, let him, Bannon concluded. There would be a time for Henry Seals.

Bannon rubbed his black mustang's neck. The horse moved smooth as silk under him, especially when going after a stray steer. He planned to switch the animal out, though, in another hour, for a fresh mount. A good cowboy didn't run his horses into the ground. He did that the first day with a bay. It was a miracle the horse didn't go lame. Reilman, the wrangler, and a black cowboy called Jackson took the young rider aside after that. They were nice about it, in spite of the wrangler's string of expletives when describing what Bannon had done. That was the beginning of a friendship between the farm boy and Jackson.

The black cowhand spoke with a Southern accent and had a thick frame that made him look shorter than his six-feet-one. His wire-rimmed spectacles and gray-speckled hair made him look older. That, and his quiet ways—and a surprising love of books. Even with his height and size, he was more impressive mentally than physically.

His round face usually had a gentle smile, with an old scratched pipe sticking out the corner of his mouth. His long, faded gray coat with the big pockets had seen a lot of drives. So had his batwing chaps and a blackish hat with a half-inch band around the wide, flat rim. A big bandanna was tied loosely at his neck. Once a rich blue, the cloth now looked like the sky on a rainy day.

Jackson carried three books in his warbag: a worn-out Bible, a collection of Tennyson's poems, and a history book. Late at night, Jackson would read by the light of a small, hand-held candle while the others slept.

Bannon caught sight of some gray shapes on the far side of the herd. That would be Freddie Tucker, red-whiskered and dull, and Israel Rankin, a former cavalry officer who walked with a bad limp. On the near side, the closest rider was Jackson in the swing-rider position. Peter Jackson was one of Dan Mitchell's most dependable men and had ridden with him on every trail drive the trail boss had made. Most of the men did not know if Jackson was his first or last name and they didn't ask. A few of the cowboys called him Black Jack, though not when he was around. He did not like his first name, so he preferred to be called Jackson.

Usually quiet around the others, Jackson and the young farm boy hit it off; the older man saw in Bannon a young man eager to learn. Bannon had never met a colored man before, but what he'd heard sure didn't fit in this man's boots. Not at all. They were already good friends. Bannon liked to listen to the older man talk about his love for books, which went beyond anything the young rider had ever experienced, especially since Bannon could barely handle printed words on cans and such. He also appreciated Jackson's sound advice.

The kid took the job of flank rider seriously, keeping steers in line without bunching or pushing them. If they got too close, cattle started stepping on each other's feet and that wasn't good. Much of the time, riding flank was boring drudgery with nothing to do but sit in a hard saddle.

About the time he relaxed, though, a steer would get the itch for something off the trail and take off. Sometimes Bannon hoped an animal would wander off just to give him something different to do. It didn't take long to discover that horses wore out faster in this position than in the drag.

That's why every man had been assigned ten good horses. His were the worst of the string, but they were solid mounts. Bannon had been the last to cut from the remuda, fitting his standing. The top riders cut their whole string at once. The rest took turns. This black was, by far, his best pick. Jackson had pointed the mount out to him.

There hadn't been time for any homesickness. Everything was new. Besides, he was too tired to think about anything after a week of sixteen-hour days in the saddle. Mitchell had pushed the cattle hard to get them away from familiar ground and the desire to wander off. He also wanted them good and tired so they would lie down at night.

These cattle were a step away from being totally wild, running free on the range until they were bunched for the northward trek. They had to be handled carefully so they would come together as if it were their own idea. Bannon had been told that the cowboys didn't really drive cattle: they just made them think a certain direction was their idea as they grazed along. The idea was to fatten them as they traveled. But it wasn't long before the herd had magically organized itself with fast walkers near the front, following the assumed leaders, and the slower "muleys," cows without horns, taking position in the rear.

"Well, Bannon, the boss'll sure know you've been working hard," John Checker's comment about the kid's muddy clothes broke into Bannon's thoughts. The point rider had greeted him as he passed, headed for the remuda and a new mount.

"Yeah . . . well . . . I guess, maybe not," the young man stammered back.

Part of his uneven response was a product of being startled, but mostly it was because of his awe of John Checker. The point rider was out of voice range before the farm boy could think of anything to say. I should have said, I just got through with my daily mud bath, he fumed to himself. Now that's what Sonny or Clanahan would have snapped back and then laughed. Checker must think I'm stupid as all get out.

Checker was as tall as Jackson, but packed lean and hard. Under his lowered wide hat brim, the man's tanned face was impossible to read most of the time. It was like he was analyzing what was inside of a man just by looking at him. An arrowhead-shaped scar on his right cheek was a reminder of a violent past, although Checker didn't talk about it.

His black hair brushed against his shoulders as he rode. Some found his face Roman in its structure, particularly the hawkish nose; women often found him handsome but usually hard to reach. Over his shirt, he wore a leather tunic taken from a Comanche warrior. Beaded and decorated with elk bone, it served as a coat except in the coldest times. Sonny Jones, the Triple C drover with the outlaw past, had observed that a man could get to a pistol faster when wearing a tunic than a regular coat.

Only the trail boss knew the real reason Checker had asked to join up—to find his sister who was now living near Dodge City. She and Checker had been separated long ago. Sometimes late at night he wondered what she'd be like and how it would be when they finally were together again. He wasn't the boy she'd remember—that was a lifetime and a lot of hard trails ago. And Amelia would not be the tearful little girl who didn't want him to leave. And made him promise that he would return for her. Why did that scene keep popping up in his mind? Still, the closer he got to Dodge City, the more his thoughts turned to Amelia. What would she look like now? What would she be like?

Most of Checker's shirts had small pinholes on the pocket from his Texas Ranger's badge. He had resigned his position and headed north to see Amelia, joining the trail drive enroute by chance. The other men thought Mr. Carlson had hired Checker to catch up with the cattle drive because a steady head—and gun—was needed to protect the herd from Indians or rustlers.

Checker had ridden into camp two weeks on the trail, and Mitchell had hired him immediately as a point rider. He knew the country and he was more than able to use a gun if that was needed. Besides, the savvy foreman liked the cut of the ranger. Soon most of the men were impressed to have him along.

The former ranger was the only hand who would look naked without a pistol belt. He wore a fancy rig, nothing like most cowhands wore. His short-barreled Colt .45 had black handles and a white elk bone circle embedded on each side. The trigger guard was half cut away, the part nearest the barrel was gone, allowing his finger to reach the trigger faster. The gun rested in a reverse-draw holster on a double cartridge belt, with a row for rifle bullets and a second one for pistol loads.

Old Peter Foster told Bannon quietly, "Checker's a man who's seen trouble and trouble ran like hell to git away. Heard tell, Clay Allison hisself done crawfished when they met. Down El Paso way, it were. Hell of a ranger, boy. Good to have 'im with us, that's fer damn sure. Best to be on his side when the lead starts flyin'."

But Jackson had put it best when he told the farm boy, "Tyrel, there's a sayin' down near the border—in order for a man to be a Texas Ranger, he's got to ride like a Mexican, track like a Comanche, shoot like a Kentuckian, and fight like the devil. I think that pretty well describes John Checker from what I hear."

Although Checker's words often had an edge to them, like he expected to be obeyed, he never talked tough—to anyone. He kept his thoughts to himself most of the time, but his eyes carefully took in everything around him. When he did speak, it was usually to Dan Mitchell or Jake Woodman, the other point rider. And usually about the drive. Occasionally Checker and Sonny Jones chatted as well. Bannon wondered why a lawman and an outlaw would be friendly. Maybe the stories about Jones weren't true.

Brushing at the drying mud on his shirt, Bannon didn't notice the trail boss coming at him from the interior of the herd. Dan Mitchell was a cowman through and through, tucked inside a wiry, average-sized frame without an ounce of fat. Jackson had described him once as a man who could read a trail brand from fifty yards, pick out the best cutting horse from a new string with one good look, handle men with little more than a glance, use a rope like it was part of his arm, or cook up a meal, if need be, in the middle of a howling thunderstorm. Bannon liked that description and he liked the trail boss.

Mitchell knew cattle and horses and understood the men who handled them. Slump-shouldered and balding, he looked like he'd been married to the prairie, putting up with her short temper, all his life. His face was tanned and he wore a thick mustache. His jutted-out chin and gray stubble made him look older than he probably was. His thin nose carried the record of several breaks and the sign of a man who'd seen trouble of all kinds and just kept coming at it. The rest of Mitchell's face was a mess of squint lines and a lopsided grin, made more so by the constant puffed-out side of his mouth holding his chewing tobacco.

When walking, the trail boss reminded Bannon of what

a sailor must look like going across the deck of a ship. That's how much the bowlegged man rocked from side to side. A slight limp was also noticeable, especially when he was tired. Bannon had never seen him without his heavy chaps and spurs. Mitchell favored a wide orange scarf and a dark cloth vest—and was rarely without a leather coat that carried many a tale of sweat, rain, and dirt.

For Mitchell's part, he was growing to like the young man, too. Where young Tyrel Bannon was short on knowing, he was long on staying put until he did. Dan Mitchell was impressed by Bannon's grit. His promotion to flank rider was Mitchell's way of saying he was pleased with his progress.

"Well, I see what that she-cow was hollerin' at. Her calf was bogged down, was it?" Mitchell said as he cut a hunk of tobacco from the square he kept in his vest. He rolled the new piece around in his mouth until it found a comfortable spot.

"Yeah," the young rider said, grinning. He was embarrassed by his appearance.

"Calf solid?"

"Looked mighty strong to me," Bannon replied, "especially when he gave me a yank."

"Yeah, they'll do that," Mitchell said with a chuckle, letting go with a string of early tobacco juice. "No other way to get 'em out. A good cowboy takes care o' the little ones. They're the next herd. Good work."

Mitchell clucked to his horse and rode off toward the chuck wagon, parallel to the herd, a few hundred yards out. The young rider reminded him of his young brother who had died at Gettysburg. Always ready to tackle anything, always eager to make the right things happen, Justis had left this world much too soon. Memories of his late brother had been pushed down inside the trail boss's mind until Tyrel Bannon brought them back. Instead of being resistant, Mitchell found himself welcoming the memory.

He smiled to himself as he told his horse to whoa so he could check some things with the cook, Tug.

Bannon felt much better as well: he could look at his muddy shirt and chaps as a badge of honor. He watched the trail boss for another instant. Mitchell was a patient man, Bannon thought. The only time Mitchell had gotten peeved at him—so it showed anyway—was at the end of the second day. Bannon had dismounted close to the bedded herd.

Dan Mitchell's words were a lesson he'd never forget: "Ty, a hoss shakin' its saddle—after you're off—can be all it takes to start a stampede. Don't do that again." Bannon had led his tired horse away, feeling very foolish.

If there was anyone he wanted to please, it was Dan Mitchell.

Something about the land they were passing made him think of home; it popped into his mind without warning. Those warm thoughts came like that sometimes, he guessed. It was the first time he'd been away from their homestead for more than one night.

Each time the thought of home came, it was sweet and more than a little painful. He was beginning to realize how tough it had been for his mother after his father and big brother died, leaving her with himself and two little sisters to feed and all.

Ahead, three steers took off to the left. That jolted him out of his bittersweet reverie. From behind him somewhere, Captain yapped and ran after them, barely more than a whirl of dust. Bannon spurred the black and followed the dog's lead, glad to be doing and not thinking.

He cleared the gulley and eased up the embankment, and there it was. He saw a buffalo that looked to him to be bigger than a house! It must be three times bigger than a regular buffalo! He laid his hand gently against the black's neck to keep it from spooking. But the animal seemed unaware of this giant in front of them.

But after Bannon blinked his eyes to clear the dust, the

monstrous buffalo was gone. Gone. Disappeared. Only three steers grazing. Bannon shook his head in disbelief. He had just seen his first mirage. He could hardly wait to tell Jackson. Almost every night a drover talked about seeing a mirage, but he would share this one only with Jackson. He'd had enough jawing on him for one day.

CHAPTER 2

RED STREAKS IN the graying sky signaled dusk. The coming break in the day was welcomed. They had made almost twenty miles. An excellent stretch. The herd had been circling slowly for at least a half hour, guided by its riders, in the nightly ritual to bring the animals into a comfortable bedding.

Well over seven acres were covered with Triple C beeves grazing and walking easily. Gradually the riders were closing the circle, though careful not to make the circle too tight. All of the riders, including Mitchell, were in sight now, bringing the herd to its evening rest. The trail boss never seemed to give any orders. Didn't have to. The crew, with the exception of Tyrel Bannon, knew what to do and did it without prompting.

Jackson swung by Bannon and said, "Don't let 'em think you're pushing them. Let 'em enjoy freedom." Jackson galloped past him, headed for a white-faced steer with one twisted horn. It had never settled down last night, keeping other animals on edge.

Tossing its head back and forth, the steer was clearing a path for itself toward the bed ground. A cow pushed her calf away from the troublemaker's swinging head. Bannon recognized the pair as his mud bog friends from this morning.

From another direction, Jake Woodman, the painstakingly accurate point rider, was headed for the same animal. Likely it would be taken out of the herd and destroyed. A single troublemaker like that could start a stampede.

Everything about a trail drive took patience, Bannon

realized. Especially when it came to these steers without horns. He clucked to a group of muleys to get them moving again. They absolutely wouldn't go into the compact herd until the others went down, no matter what. And they were always the first in the morning to rise and move on, before their horned counterparts did so.

"Bullheads" was Dan Mitchell's favorite term for them. Muleys were more trouble than horned animals because they tended to jam together, so they suffered more from the heat and lost weight easily. Bannon yipped and slapped his lariat against his chaps to get their attention. Pieces of dried mud sprinkled around his legs.

His voice and manner were forced. It still embarrassed him to hear his own thin voice above the other noises. The rest of the drovers had calls that sounded more in control and forceful, more like men.

The young rider tried his best to keep the muleys from crowding each other. His black took easily to jamming its heavy body alongside any steer that needed special attention. Bannon had decided the horse hated cattle and liked trying to lean against them or cut them off.

His main task, like everyone else's, was to see that all the animals bedded down with plenty of room between bodies. One tail slapping another's face could be enough to send a cow into a bawling fury and the whole herd would be off—so Bannon had been told. His weariness was clear to the bone and he was ready for supper; their noon meal had been a can of cold beans in the saddle.

Everything about this camp was good: elevation, grass, water, and wood for cooking. The next step was to move the cattle up to the bed ground for the night. It had been chosen by Mitchell to provide every advantage of elevation. Bannon moved slowly with the tightening herd, imitating the others. Most of the animals would end up picking matted grass to lie on, so the milling was creating an attractive bed.

Off to the side was Dan Mitchell on a tall bay, doing what he did every night: counting the herd. He moved small pebbles from one coat pocket to the other, one for each hundred as it was accounted for. Bannon watched out of the corner of his eye. He hoped the tally was right. If they'd lost any, somebody would have to go back for the strays. Probably him. If there were too many, it meant range cattle had drifted in and someone had to cut them out. Mitchell was strong on that. The young rider realized he had never seen the trail boss leave the herd at dusk until the beeves had bedded down and the first guards were in place.

From across a span of twenty steers, Seals yelled, "Come on, Bannon! Git your beeves movin' with the rest of us. We don't want to be doin' this all night. For chrissakes! Damn greenhorn."

The words were barely out of his mouth when Seals's horse stumbled from fatigue and caught itself. That was enough for the cowboy's anger to explode. Viciously, he spurred and yelled at the animal, yanking hard on the bit as he unleashed his fury. Out of nowhere came Mitchell's rope, out so quickly Bannon didn't see the movement. In a blink, the guilty cowboy was on the ground, sucking air with the foreman's rope tight around his chest. Cattle milled past him, ignoring the downed man.

His horse was trotting free, stirrups dancing in rhythm, unsettled by it all. Not a word was spoken by Mitchell or Seals or anyone else. The lesson was clear. The trail boss didn't have much tolerance for a man who would hit his horse when angry. Brushing himself off as he stood up, Seals glanced toward Bannon and glared. He didn't look at Mitchell, who had ridden away to talk with John Checker, coiling up his rope as he rode. Bannon allowed himself a small smile before going back to his chore.

Near the chuck wagon, Reilman the wrangler was putting up his rope corral to hold the horses for the night.

His triangular pen was installed in minutes: one end of the rope was tied to the back wagon wheel, the other to the far lip of the wagon tongue, and the middle pulled back to stakes driven in the ground.

Helping him was the calf wagon driver, Stuart Willis. A frail, white-haired gentleman, Willis had been a hand with the Triple C for many winters. His wagon load of twenty-eight unstable calves had been allowed to return to their mothers for the evening. A practical decision. The noise they would make all night, along with their mothers, would keep everyone awake. Getting a few hours of peaceful sleep was worth the trouble of rounding them up in the morning.

The wagon itself said a mouthful about Dan Mitchell. A lot of trail bosses wouldn't mess with young stuff. Thought it held them back. If calves couldn't keep up, they were left behind to die. Jackson told Bannon that Mitchell always ran a calf wagon and usually sold the calves to a local rancher after selling the main herd.

Most of the horses had been broken to camp life on the move. But some would need hobbling. Willis's soft voice and gentle ways were a warm contrast to Reilman's loud and constant swearing, as the two brought the string of mustangs under control for the evening. Only a few night horses would be needed for the guards.

Across the way, the cook had cornered Sonny Jones for a project. Wearing his dusty derby and narrowed-legged shotgun chaps, Sonny was one of Tug's favorites. Of course, Sonny was liked by everyone on the drive. Always smiling, always laughing, Sonny seemed to have a private joke going on with the day, every day. When he wasn't laughing, he was singing. There was a good likelihood Sonny Jones was somebody else in South Texas, somebody wanted by the law. But nobody cared. Especially not Tug, who had the evening meal well underway. At first, Sonny Jones was uneasy around Checker. But the ranger had sought him out early on, and they had been friendly to each other ever since.

Everyone had called him by his nickname Tug for so many years he probably wouldn't recognize his real name if someone addressed him as Ernest Leonard Jamison. The nickname came from a happening long ago, at another ranch, when Tug wouldn't let a cowhand take a freshly baked pie and "tugged" on it until the man got disgusted and gave up. Tug had worked for the Triple C for eight years. And this was his eighth drive with Dan Mitchell as trail boss. Only Jackson had been around longer.

Tug was a funny-looking mixture of a man: stumpy, bald, with a full beard of striking shades of silver, black, and red. He walked as if his legs were mismatched. And his face had tanned so deeply, he'd still be brown after living on the North Pole for a year.

Tug was hard of hearing and usually got some but not all of what others were saying. Even Dan Mitchell occasionally lost his temper at Tug's always asking for a repeat of what had just been said.

"Sonny, got me a glimpse of a farm back yonder. Remember that big rock, the one looked like a bear?" Tug asked as he stirred a bowl of biscuit dough. From his saddle, Sonny nodded and grinned, waiting for the request he knew was coming.

"Take this here sack o' coins an' see if you kin buy some eggs. Butter'd be nice."

Sonny accepted the small sack and stuffed it in an already crowded vest pocket. Nobody packed more things into a vest than this happy man. Matches, makin's, cartridges, and a handful of long leather strips. A few pieces of hard candy too. There was also an old watch; its cover held a cracked photograph of a young woman he never talked about.

"How about some bear sign too?" Sonny suggested with a wink.

"What?"

"Bear sign. You know, donuts."

"Yeah, by the rock. Maybe a half mile."

"No, donuts, Tug. Donuts," Sonny tried to explain, his words louder and more slowly this time.

"Oh, bear sign! Why didn't ya say so before!" Tug growled. "Good idea. A apple pie or two would be nice too."

Sonny laughed, wheeled his horse, nudged it with his spurs, and galloped away. His shirttail flapped in the wind, out like it usually was.

A few minutes later, Tyrel Bannon cantered up to the chuck wagon. Mitchell had sent him, at Tug's request. The greenhorn had become another of the cook's favorites. Bannon could be counted on to shoot prairie chickens or grouse every time he went out. Whatever he shot became breakfast and a nice change of pace from beef and salt pork.

Tug's prized double-barreled shotgun was offered as if a treasure by the salty cook. The young rider took it and headed out toward a distant treeline to the east. Tug didn't even give him suggestions anymore on where to look. Back home, bullets were too scarce around the Bannon household not to hit what was aimed at. And it was rare his mother's table was without meat that he had bagged.

Bannon's only other weapon was an old Army Colt .44 that took powder, percussion caps, and ball. Even when loaded, it could misfire with the worst of them. The pistol had been his father's. A holster was made out of an old piece of harness just for the drive. There was comfort in its silent weight at his hip.

Before the drive started, Mitchell initially had a negative reaction to his even bringing a gun. He warned that one bullet fired could send an entire herd into flight. When Bannon unbuckled his pistol belt to leave it, the trail boss asked to see how well he could shoot. Bannon showed him, busting three rocks into shreds from twenty-five yards with three quick shots. Mitchell had grinned wide and told him to wear it.

The young rider had no rifle; most of the men did, either a Henry or a Winchester. Mitchell, Seals, Checker, and Sonny carried the new Winchester 73 model. So did Tex, the handsome cowboy with stars on his chaps and shirts. Even the stock of his Winchester featured a carved version. Bannon's mother had tried to give him their Henry, the one with the awkward loading tube, to take along, but he wouldn't hear of it.

Often he wished for one of those new cartridge-loading Colts like everyone else on the drive wore, except him and the old timer, Pete Foster, a grizzled cowboy with a huge mustache.

"Bannon," Foster had told the farm boy, "onliest thing a six-shooter's fer is to git rid o' rattlesnakes . . . or cut down a hoss draggin' ya. So this here hoss pistol is just fine. Can't hit anythin' with 'em, anyway."

"One of them new 'chesters would be mighty fine too," Bannon said to himself. The black twisted its ears to determine the conversation's content. "Maybe I can get one—or a Colt—when we get to Dodge. Maybe I'll have enough to do that. Still have plenty to bring home n' all."

Getting away from the drudgery of the saddle would be a relief. But it also meant he had the graveyard watch, the last guard before hitting the trail in the morning. Anyone on that shift went right into the drive without sleeping again. Probably him, Jackson, Wonson, and Foster.

"I won't come back empty," he said to himself as he searched for wild game. He spit out his self-determination, then looked down at his mud-streaked shirt and chaps. Their appearance made him more determined. Tonight, in the stream, they could be cleaned. The shirt was one of two he had with him. The chaps needed special caring for; they weren't his. Mr. Carlson had lent them to him for the drive, along with a pair of old spurs and a new rope.

From the edge of the nearly settled herd, Checker rolled a smoke, licked the loose flap, and sealed it with his fingers. He watched everything unfold around him, like a panther surveying his land. Pale blue eyes, eyes that could pierce a man's soul, had observed both Sonny and Bannon leaving, as well as Jackson and Woodman taking the twisted-horn steer over the ridge.

Nothing looked out of place; no steers appeared to be unnerved by the stopping. They had been given a good watering just an hour ago, so they should be ready for bed. But one never knew with cattle. Checker struck a match against the butt of his pistol. Inhaling, he let a string of white smoke whisper slowly into the gray air. Figuring what a steer was going to do was harder than figuring what a man was going to do. He could read men. Cattle—and women—were something else.

Riding up to him now was the trail boss. Mitchell respected the gunfighter's trail-driving skills—and his judgment—enough to make him one of the two point riders for the drive.

"What do you think, John?" Mitchell asked, smiling, as he pulled up alongside the silent ranger.

"Good day, boss. Damn good day."

"Yeah, we'll hit the Wichita easy tomorrow."

"Yeah," Checker responded, smoke curling around his hard face. "Will she be angry?"

"Heard tell Shanghai Pierce took a big herd across it only a week back. It was high."

"Hell, them Matagorda steers of his—they can swim across anything."

"Yeah, heard tell he calls them his sea lions"—Mitchell took a bag of Bull Durham from his shirt pocket and began to make a cigarette—"right from the Gulf of Mexico."

Both men chuckled. Then the former ranger asked how many herds the trail boss figured were ahead of them on the Western Trail into Kansas. Mitchell thought three at the most.

"Well, so far they've left us plenty of grass," the point rider responded.

"An' water."

"Yeah, praise 'em for that," Checker said, placing his hand on the trail boss's shoulder to emphasize his point.

Mitchell nodded, took off his sweat-stained wide-brimmed hat and wiped his forehead with his sleeve. "Every night I do" was the unexpected reply.

"Are you going to scout a crossing?" Checker asked, "or do you want Woodman—or . . ."

"You know this land. Why don't you do it?"

"Okay." Checker accepted the task with little emotion in his face. He took a watch from his vest pocket and popped open the silver lid. On the inside of the watch cover was a tiny cracked photograph of a woman with two small children, a boy and a younger girl. "Dan, there's two hours of daylight. Anything you need doing?"

"Nope, we're in good shape. I'm gonna break myself as soon as Foster and the others take guard," Mitchell answered, staring at the smoke from his fresh-lit cigarette. "Take a breather. You've earned it." He settled his hat back on his head.

"Thanks, but I'm gonna scout over north there for a piece."

"Lookin' for water?"

"No, Woodman's got us covered for water the next few days. I'm looking for Kiowas."

"Kiowas? They're two days away, on the other side of the Red." Mitchell glanced up quickly, his eyes flashing.

"I hope you're right," Checker responded, his own eyes

surveying the ocean of quieting animals. "But I heard some were off the reservation. Heard they got a herd like ours. A month ago. Killed every man jack. If I swing wide, I might find tracks."

"Or the goddamned savages themselves."

Jake Woodman rode over to join them. A top rider and a fine trail maker, he was the other point rider Mitchell depended upon. Woodman was an intense man who chewed on every detail and watched everything around him. Everything. If asked, he could probably recall the exact number of scrub oak the herd passed during the morning.

He was always worried about something, no matter how good the day was. He worried when the herd lay down during the day to rest, which was often, that the drovers wouldn't be able to get the beeves moving again. He worried when the steers got up too fast, or wouldn't go down in the first place because they were too thirsty. He worried when they crowded each other and when they got too spread out. Particularly, he worried when the drive was out of sight of water. Which was most of the time. And most of the time, he worried about his feet. Without a word to each other, both Mitchell and Checker had decided not to mention the possibility of Kiowas in the area.

"Hello, Jake," Checker greeted him warmly. "Another good day."

"Well, I don't know, Checker. I think they're lookin' a little thin. Don't you?" Woodman responded, his forehead furrowed in concern. "An' my feet are hurting," he groaned, pointing to his boots. "Must be my socks. Didn't get them on right this morning. Been bothering me all day."

Mitchell nodded, a smile trying to break through his wrinkled face. Checker looked down at the ground, then rubbed his hand across his mouth, trying to hide the same response. The three men parted after that: Mitchell, to see if the first assigned guards were in place; Checker, to scout the area ahead; Woodman, to change his socks and begin his nightly ritual of working on a piece of tack. Tonight his saddle was due for soaping.

It was slap-dark when Bannon returned from his hunting trip. Sonny had come back an hour earlier; two dozen eggs, a jar of plum jam, and a sack of corn mush were his purchased trophies.

Eight birds were strung over Bannon's shoulder. More impressive was a dead buck deer slung across his saddle. Tug received them all with his usual grunt, along with the return of his shotgun. He examined the weapon to assure no harm had come to it. Then he realized the young rider had downed a deer without a rifle.

"How'd the hell you stop this here buck, Tyrel?" he exclaimed.

"Caught him waterin'. Easy enough shot."

"With that side arm?"

"Well . . . yessir."

"Hot damn, boy. We're gonna put you in the same kettle with Checker and Sonny. Pistoleros, that's what. Are ya hungry?"

"Mighty, Tug."

After eating the supper set aside for him, the young rider went to the stream and washed out his shirt and the bandanna around his neck. Silently he was thankful his mother had found some light brown cloth to use for the neckerchief, instead of the red gingham she had first suggested. He didn't need to stick out any more than by his own doing.

Jake Woodman was at the stream washing his feet. "That black hoss workin' good for you, Bannon?" the point rider asked and, without waiting for an answer, continued. "How's that saddle? Man can't take too good a care of his leather. Soapin' mine tonight. Got some wear on the cinch. May change it out. Have you checked yours?"

Bannon started to answer, but Woodman continued, "Gonna be hittin' the Wichita tomorrow. That could be god-almighty rough. Make sure you're ridin' your river hoss. Usin' that big dun for that, aren't ya?"

He worried aloud about the weather, the next water, the next bed ground, and then back to horses, saddles, ropes, gloves, boots—and, finally, to feet. Bannon didn't mind hearing about the first handful of subjects: Woodman knew a lot that he didn't. But he drew the line on feet.

"You know, a fella ought to rub his feet for a half hour," Woodman said. "Every night. Had a doctor in Kansas City tell me that. Wash 'em every chance you get. Change your socks every day. Add years."

When Woodman paused to take a breath, Bannon excused himself, saying he needed to help clean the game he'd brought in. Anything was better than listening to Woodman and his damned feet.

As he walked away in the dark, he muttered to himself, "Wonder if he knows I've only got one pair of socks. Hell, I'd rather have blisters than sit around rubbing my feet. Man, that's pitiful."

The night hung everywhere as he returned to camp and sought out Tug. The feisty cook didn't want his help with the game and told him to relax. Bone tired, he saw the yellow glow of the campfire, heard the soft melody of men's voices. Tug handed him a steaming cup of coffee. It tasted fine, but the hot metal burned his fingers. Shaking his hand to relieve the sting, he half fell over the wagon's tongue but caught himself, spilling most of the coffee.

The heavy tongue was pointed the way the herd would head tomorrow. Dan Mitchell set his direction by the North Star each evening, then had the chuck wagon set in the right angle for the morning's drive. Mitchell's own night horse was saddled, picketed close to where he was already sleeping. Another nightly procedure. Mitchell and Tug were always the first up. (Bannon wondered, sometimes, if the cook ever went to sleep. He was always awake, it seemed.) Sometimes the trail boss himself led the herd out at dawn, letting the point riders have some extra breakfast time.

Embarrassed by stumbling over the wagon's tongue, Bannon returned to the coffeepot and refilled his cup. Tug was dressing out the deer and didn't notice.

"Where you been, Ty? Been looking all over for you, boy." It was Jackson, smoking a pipe.

The two friends joined the hands who were sitting around the campfire. Talk quickly came around to the young man's recent accuracy with a gun.

"Tug's been a-whippin' up a tale that you done bagged a buck . . . with that ol' iron on your hip, Bannon," Foster said, a quizzical look in his eyes.

"Yeah, and the darlin' said you be a-bringing it in with a bunch of birds, you did," added Clanahan. "Two holes in the buck's head. Sure as the mornin'."

Bannon wasn't certain what to say. So he said nothing.

The gimpy-legged Israel Rankin asked how big a rack the buck had.

Seals couldn't miss the opportunity to ridicule. "Hard to believe a ranny who can't stay out of the mud could shoot anything. Just don't fire that old musket while you're nighthawkin', boy. We don't want to have to clean up another mess of yours."

"Goddammit! Leave Bannon alone," Reilman spat. "You're the sorry sonofabitch that got yanked off his hoss today. Not him."

Seals jumped to his feet, his hand moving to the pistol at his side.

"Don't," Sonny commanded. His eyes cornered Seals and waited for his next action. Nothing moved. No one spoke.

Jackson's words were soothing. "Long day, boys. Long day. Bannon got us some fine eatin' for tomorrow. Don't go spoiling it with a fuss over nothing."

"Sorry, Sonny. Randy, sorry. Just tired, that's all." Seals finally defused the moment, his hands rising slowly toward his shirt pocket and the tobacco plug waiting there. Then he walked away.

Gradually the comfort came back to the fire, but the young rider felt frustrated. Others had stepped in where he should have stepped. Maybe Seals wasn't going to let him be until he stood up to him.

Tex, the handsome cowboy who liked looking at himself in the little mirror he carried, returned to the subject, "I wonder if Checker has ever killed a deer with a pistol. Have you, Sonny?"

"No. Have not," the happy cowboy answered in a sing-song voice, "but I've sure thrown lead at 'em with a rifle. Ka-bing! Ka-bam!"

Everyone laughed. Louder and longer than the remark deserved. When the response had settled into renewed contemplation, Sonny asked the young rider about his feat, "How far away were you, Ty?"

"Oh, no more than twenty-two, twenty-four yards. Came up on it at a pond. Drinkin'. Wasn't much of a shot."

"How many times did you shoot?"

"Well, twice actually. Shot the first time and it took off a-running. So I upped and fired again. First one had him, though. He woulda stopped in his tracks in another step or two. I just got anxious."

"Did you hit it on the run?" Sonny asked, fascinated by the young man's ability and his lack of arrogance about it.

"Yeah, but didn't need to. Shouldn't have wasted the shot."

Freddie Tucker stirred the dying fire with a stick and changed the topic to tomorrow's river. His description of a previous crossing gave Bannon the shivers.

After a few minutes, Bannon excused himself and headed for his blankets. The night would be short enough. Approaching hoofbeats caught his ear and he turned to see who it was. The campfire's glow caught the face of the rider. John Checker. Where had he been?

Bannon watched the tall man go directly to the trail boss. The ranger rolled a smoke as he made a brief report. Evidently it wasn't good news, because Mitchell grimaced. They contined to talk, but Bannon lay down and covered himself with his blanket. A gauzy picture of himself, his father, and his brother came floating into his tired mind. What would his father or his brother have done with someone like Seals?

Seems like all I do is learn, he thought. Probably I should be paying them for the teachin'. This is my first trail drive and it shows, too much of the time. The only thing I know much about is farming. Enough to know I don't want to be one.

"Listen to this," Jackson said quietly to Bannon, interrupting his reverie without realizing it. The black man was curled up in his blankets and reading with a candle.

" 'His broad clear brow in sunlight glow'd;/On burnishe'd hooves his war-horse trode;/From underneath his helmet flow'd/His coal black curls as on he rode,/As he rode to Camelot.' "

"That's mighty pretty, Jackson," Bannon said, not really knowing what to say, "who did the writin'?"

"Oh, that's Tennyson. Alfred Lord Tennyson. That's a piece of his writin', *The Revenge*. He likes to write about fightin'."

"Anything in there about a fella named Seals?"

Jackson chuckled. So did the young farm boy. Then both looked over at Checker's bedroll twenty yards away, where the ranger had just laid down. They saw him take an envelope from his shirt pocket. He pulled several sheets from it, opened them reverently, and began reading, holding the letter in one hand and a short piece of candle in the other. They'd seen him read that same letter a dozen times since they left.

"There's a man with a big hole in his heart, Tyrel," Jackson said softly. "An' he's praying she'll fill it."

"Checker's got a woman waiting for him . . . in Dodge?"

"A real special one. His sister. Haven't seen each other since they were kids."

Tyrel Bannon was silent for a moment as the significance of his friend's words registered,

"Jackson, how'd you come to know this?" He wasn't questioning his truthfulness; it just seemed like Checker wasn't the kind to talk about himself much.

"Told me about it this morning. That's why he's riding with us. Mostly. He's all excited. Inside. Worried too. Like an old woman." Jackson continued, glancing over at Checker, "Hard to believe, isn't it? Here's a man who's faced just about everything bad Texas can throw at a man—and he's worried about seeing his sister."

"Yeah, it is," Bannon said, not daring to look at the ranger.

"I didn't ask him why they were separated back then. Figured he'd tell me if he wanted to," Jackson said, anticipating Bannon's unstated question. "Doesn't pay to go nosing along a man's backtrail uninvited. Especially one like Checker. I don't plan on telling anybody, except you. You shouldn't either."

"Oh, I won't."

Checker was again consumed by the soft, curved handwriting that pulled him back to the past, one that he had shoved away. The envelope was addressed to "Mister John Checker, Texas Rangers, Fort Worth, Texas." The letter said,

> Dear Johnny,
> My hopes and prayers are that you are well. I can only pray that this letter comes into your hands. Not a day has passed that my prayers have not been of you.

My dear husband, Orville, has warned me not to expect to see you again. He does not want to see me hurt. I know that is why he has said this. I pray this letter finds you. My others have not, I fear.

My heart jumped so high when I overheard a Texas cowboy mention your name. I was in town doing my weekly trading when a man told one of the store clerks that none of the Kansas lawmen could hold a candle to Texas Rangers like John Checker. I dropped my basket when I heard your name. I thought I was going to faint.

The cowboy helped me pick up my goods and I asked him to tell me about you. He told me he had seen you last in Fort Worth.

I am hoping and praying this will find its way to you. I told him that you sounded like a friend of my husband's. I thought this was better than saying what was in my heart, that my brother had been found at long last.

The last news we had of you was years ago. Someone said, and I am reluctant to even write the words, that you were an outlaw and had been killed a long time ago with a gang of bank robbers over in Ellsworth. How silly that sounds now, knowing you are a peace officer . . .

The letter had been written over a year ago. Her married name was Hedrickson now. She and her husband, Orville, had an eight-year-old son named Johnny. Every time Checker thought about his namesake, the honor thrilled him. Amelia also had a baby girl, Rebecca. They had dairy cows, grew some corn, and Orville broke horses for selling. The letter was filled with details of their lives, particularly of her children. Amelia had invited him to come and visit them at their homestead, a day's ride south of Dodge City. She'd even included a hand-drawn map. She reminded him of his promise to come back to her when he rode out fifteen years ago.

The idea of seeing her had simmered inside him for months. Finally he had made up his mind, resigned his position, and headed north. Although he was anxious to see Amelia and her family, he was reluctant to revisit the past.

Their father had been J. D. McCallister, a notorious saloon keeper in Dodge's rough-and-tumble, buffalo-hunting days. He had never married their mother nor recognized the children as his, wedding another woman instead. McCallister's son by this woman was about Amelia's age.

His saloon was constructed of chinked walls, canvas roof, dirt floor, and wicked whiskey. But it was mainly known as a place to stay away from. Unwary customers, if lucky, found themselves the next day in an alley with sore heads and empty purses. The unlucky ones were hauled out of town during the night by McCallister's ruffian friends, their dead bodies dumped in a washout. There were also rumors of buried bodies in a backyard coal shed.

J. D. McCallister had left Checker, his sister, and their mother in poverty without even a goodbye. A few years later, Checker's mother died of whooping cough when he was fourteen and Amelia was eight. Pictures of that awful time, when neighbors took his sister in and he left for good, haunted him every time he read the rest of Amelia's letter:

J. D. McCallister died ten years ago. He and his gang were shot and his saloon burned down. His son Star is as different from his father as you are. He is a successful saloon owner in Dodge. But that is as close as the similarity gets. I've talked with him several times and he is very nice. His father's deeds embarrassed him greatly. I think you would like him.

After all these years, he was returning home, home to his sister, his only family. Was he being foolish? He blew out the candle and replaced the letter in the envelope. A fitful sleep took him away to a place where gunfire was a constant and he could never quite get to his little sister or his mother.

CHAPTER 3

R-R-R-R-R-R-R-R-R-R-R-R-R-R-R-R-R. BANNON LAY on his side, instantly awake, but unmoving. His mind recognized that terrifying rattle even as he slept. A rattlesnake! Behind him and near his head.

R-r-r-r-r-r-r-r-r-r. He froze, trying to think. Movement could bring its strike. Would his blanket be thick enough to withstand the venomous fangs? He tried to ease the fear within him. He'd been around rattlers before. Stay calm. Stay calm. He inched his arm out of the blanket until he could reach one of his boots. The rattler must not see or sense any sign of movement under the blanket.

One knee rested on the upper leather of the boot. Within easy reach. Be patient. R-r-r-r-r-r-r-r-r-r-r. Maybe he could slam it down on the snake before the creature struck. Maybe the spur itself would help. Even if he missed, it might knock the snake off balance for an instant. He'd use his blanket to smother it. R-r-r-r-r-r-r-r-r-r-r-r-r-r.

Slam! In one smooth motion, his boot and spur came down hard where he thought the snake was curled. The slap of his blanket followed to smother the danger. Someone cried out. And Bannon jumped free. Throughout the sleeping camp, men jumped to their feet in response to the yell. Some grabbed guns. Others ran toward Bannon, shaking off sleep as they came.

Gripping his bleeding hand with his other was Wonson. Bannon had caught the cowboy's hand good and deep. Seals stood next to the wounded prankster, his mouth open in astonishment. Beside both men was a dropped can, now half-filled with rocks. More pebbles were strewn about the damp ground. A few were atop Bannon's boot. The spur glistened with dots of red. Wonson and Seals had sneaked up on the young rider with the idea of making him think a rattlesnake was next to him by shaking a can filled with small stones.

"What's going on?" demanded Reilman, the first to get there.

"Oh, this dumb kid just upped and jabbed Wonson with his spur as he went by. Damn fool!" Seals gestured toward Bannon as he spoke.

"Hell, what kind of a windy you spinning here, Seals?" Pete Foster eased between Seals and Reilman, his old Army Colt at his side. "Looks to me like you two tried to make the kid here think he was being attacked by a rattler. Yessir, that's what it was—"

"Indeed, an' the young lad out-pranked you, he did," completed Harry Clanahan, beginning to laugh. Bannon stood, unmoving, in his long underwear. Unsure of what to say or do.

Soon the whole camp was roaring with laughter at the prank misfiring. Clanahan bandaged the cut on Wonson's hand. Of course, the Irishman's continuous chuckling over the matter made it take longer.

It seemed to Bannon that every other night, Seals and others tried a different way to upset him. The pranks had grown tiresome, adding to Bannon's feeling that he wouldn't ever be a real part of the drive. But he was certain Seals kept it going long after anyone else wanted to.

In the morning dampness, Henry Seals's hateful stare took on an added dimension of cruelty. He shook his head at Wonson, the cohort he had talked into the prank, and walked away.

Bannon apologized, "Sorry, Wonson . . . I didn't know it was you. Honest." The young rider's face was full of concern.

Gradually, men went back to their bedrolls to dress for

the day. Somewhere in the grayness, someone said, "They're gonna push that kid too far and have hell to pay." It was Checker talking to Sonny.

"Damn fools are lucky the kid didn't grab that ol' Colt," Sonny responded, his eyes twinkling. His right hand rested on the butt of his pistol. He, Checker, Mitchell, Woodman, and Tug were the only ones dressed. Sonny's derby was cocked forward on his head as if he had tried to put it on and almost missed.

Checker grunted and turned to check his horse, standing behind him. Like Mitchell, he always kept his fastest mount saddled and near him at night. The black belonged to Checker, not to the remuda. Methodically, he examined each hoof, using a small pocketknife to remove mud and rock.

"The kid's got sand," Sonny continued, glancing under his hat brim at the gunfighter with his back toward him. "Lot more'n most. I don't care if he's green. He's learnin'. An' fast."

"Yeah. Seals isn't readin' the signs. That kid's gonna tear him apart one of these days. Wait an' see." Checker let the back leg down after his inspection. He pulled a sack of Bull Durham from his vest pocket as he swung back around to Sonny.

"Can you believe that tale about the buck?" Sonny asked. "You think he can shoot like that?"

Checker thought for a moment as he completed the cigarette and stuck it in his mouth, "I think he can shoot like that. If the Kiowas come, that farm boy will be right handy." He popped a match on the butt of his gun and drew the flame into the tightly rolled tobacco.

"You see anything last night?" Sonny asked, in response to the last comment.

"Found the camp of another big herd. East of here. Two miles maybe. Cross T, from down around Fort Still."

Checker was talking low enough that only Sonny could

hear. "Said they got hit by a war party. North side of the Wichita. Ran off a hundred head. Killed a drover."

"Before the Nations?"

"Before the Nations."

Checker quietly explained he had also seen tracks of unshod ponies on both sides of the river. He had advised Mitchell of his findings last night. The trail boss said he would announce the sighting after they crossed the river. Everybody would be told to carry his rifle and keep a good horse saddled and by his bed.

Woodman came over to tell Checker what he had already seen for himself. The herd was getting restless. It wouldn't be the first time the herd started moving before the crew was ready. The two point riders decided to grab what they could to eat and down it in the saddle. That way they could get in front of the animals and keep them from drinking. Mitchell wouldn't want them to be watered this morning, to help make them ready for the crossing.

"Got brand-new socks on this morning," Woodman said, beaming. "Bought 'em before we left. Boy, they feel great. Washed 'em twice just to break 'em in."

Breakfast was nearly ready. The morning sun was barely streaking across the dark sky as Checker and Woodman came to the chuck wagon. Tug was surveying the steaming pans and pots with satisfaction. When the feisty cook was getting ready for a meal, he didn't like anyone even getting close to the wagon. Except to grab up a plate when vittles were ready—and only after he had called the hands to grub.

But he understood the two riders' need to get moving and made each one a big venison sandwich with a fried egg. Both gulped down cups of hot coffee and headed out. Woodman told the cook that the wagon would be brought across last, after the herd was in place. Tug nodded. It didn't make any difference to him. River crossings were always bad.

Since it was Bannon's good fortune that brought the deer, Tug invited him over for an early taste as well. The young cowboy was impressed. Venison, fried eggs, biscuits with plum jam. Mitchell believed in keeping his riders well fed and well mounted. Tug did a good job with the first part by anyone's standards.

Bannon filled a cup of hot coffee, letting its warmth work into his fingers. Tug was busy, finishing the meal. The young rider always took delight in discovering the many names the cook had for everything: the "wreck pan" was where dirty dishes went; the "squirrel can" was for food scraps; "Arbuckles" was his favorite name for hot coffee. That was the name on the coffee sack. Had a pretty flying angel on it, too. Came all the way from Pittsburgh.

Jackson ambled up beside Bannon, worried about his young friend's state of mind. The black cowboy was usually quiet around the others; not subservient, but definitely avoiding any unnecessary conflict. But he was fed up with Seals. It had to stop. Bannon deserved better. Maybe tonight Jackson would have a chance to talk with Checker about it. If anyone could shut up Seals it would be Checker.

To make the young rider feel better, Jackson told him a funny story about Tug and his lack of hearing.

"Must've been a year ago, yeah, at least that. Ol' Tug had a style of answering with all-purpose kinda answers to hide his not hearing so well," the black man said, smiling as he recounted the story.

"You know . . . 'that's interesting' . . . 'sure nuff' . . . 'you don't say' . . . 'seems to make sense' . . . even 'uh-huh' . . . stuff like that."

Jackson stopped and coughed to clear his throat, glancing over at Tug to make certain he didn't hear.

"Well, one day this, oh my, this homely spinster . . . at the ranch to help Missus Carlson with her cookin'. I mean she would make a drunk man sober. Well, she thought he wanted to marry her because he answered 'uh-huh' when she asked him if he thought she was pretty . . . then, then . . . she asked him if he'd ever thought about her as a wife . . . an' the old fool said, 'Seems to make sense.' "

Tears were running down Jackson's cheeks. He couldn't go on, the laughter was filling his throat. Bannon was laughing hard, too. A few minutes passed with both men unable to speak. Tug gave them a harsh look but was too busy to find out the reason for their behavior.

Finally, Jackson finished his story, "It got so bad . . . she showed up one day with a preacher at her side. An' flowers in her hand. You should've seen the look on Tug's face! I thought I was gonna die!"

Jackson shook his head, wiping his eyes with his shirt-sleeve, "No more of that bluffing for Tug. Since that day he just repeats most things a fellow says as a question, to make certain he heard right."

Bannon bit his lower lip to hold in the chuckle. The rattlesnake prank was forgotten.

Breakfast was long behind them and the morning sun was getting hot when the call came back to "squeeze 'em down." The river crossing was coming up, and the point riders wanted the herd bunched together. The Wichita!

Getting cattle to take to water took patience, even more than usual if it was swimming water. Today it was going to be swimming water. Treacherous as all hell, the veterans said. Bannon's jaw tightened a little.

One at a time, each cowboy broke from his trail position to ride to the chuck wagon. There, each man shed his chaps, pants, shirt, boots, and pistol belt, then stuffed them into his war bag and climbed back into the saddle. Hats and long johns were the uniform of the day. Sure beat wearing soaking-wet clothes. Tug would hold up the wagon on this side of the Wichita until the herd had crossed. The plan was to float it over on a raft they would make, or so Bannon had heard.

When it came Bannon's turn, he removed his clothes quickly and stuffed them into a small cloth bag. It carried the only other clothes he owned. A second pair of pants and another shirt. Others kept their war bags filled with nicer things like old letters, decks of cards, cigarette makings or maybe a photograph, or bills of sale for their own horses, or a harmonica. Most had fine going-to-town clothes for wearing to Dodge. Fancy spurs too. Two or three had catalogs from boot and saddle makers.

Bannon unbelted the heavy Colt, wrapped his belt around the handmade holster, and laid it on top of his wadded clothes. He swung up into the saddle and cantered back into position. His throat was tight. "Please don't let me foul up, Lord," he prayed.

Off to the far side Freddie Tucker and Israel Rankin were helping Randy Reilman push the remuda to get the horses in front of the cattle. Mitchell had decided to send the remount herd across the river first to make the cattle more comfortable with the crossing. Bannon could hear Sonny singing, just barely catching a few phrases against the hot afternoon air. It was a good sound, making him feel more at ease. Seemed like Sonny made up new verses every day to the same songs.

All the trail stories of vicious river crossings where men and animals had died came bouncing into his young mind. Unexpected things of every sort could kill the best of trail hands: High, rushing water could knock a man silly; undercurrents could pull a horse down and keep it there; there might be quicksand where it didn't look like there was any; you could get slammed into by steers that went crazy in the water.

Only a fool wouldn't be worried. His first river experiences had gone without any kind of a snag, but the water had been swimming depth just once and that was slow moving. The key was getting the lead steer into the water right after the mustangs; the rest of the cattle would usually follow. A big, speckled beast with the confidence of a mountain lion was the herd leader. They'd taken to calling it "John Henry."

By the time Bannon got to the mauled bank where the cattle were timidly easing into the water, Checker was leading John Henry up on the far side. Behind them a long brown stream of horns and heads snaked across the deep current. Captain was nipping at any steers hesitating. Spread-out riders were stationed downstream to keep the herd from drifting. Men were yipping and hollering in a comforting rhythm.

Dan Mitchell sat astride his horse near the south bank, counting cattle as they passed. He nodded as Bannon passed. On the far side, Woodman was doing the same.

There wasn't any sun glare off the water. Sonny Jones had told Bannon that if the sun shone in the eyes of the cattle, they had a hard time seeing the opposite bank and probably wouldn't budge. A good trail boss wouldn't try to put cattle into the water when glare was there. It was no surprise that Dan Mitchell had timed it right.

Swinging his bare right foot free of the stirrup, Bannon loosened the cinch slightly. A horse swelled when swimming, so it was wise to give it room. That's what Jackson said—and did. Giving the little dun a nudge with his heels, Bannon eased into the water and off the embankment at a point where the cattle hadn't gone. It looked less slippery, and there weren't any other animals to worry about.

Water seeped upward, cresting around his knees. Actually it felt rather good in the hot afternoon. The water grew deeper and swifter. Soon Bannon's horse was swimming. Reins don't mean a thing to a horse in water, Jackson had told him. Pulling on them was apt to cause the horse to go over backward and drown both animal and rider. Jackson had told him that the best way to guide a horse was with gentle slaps on the neck or to splash water in his face opposite the direction desired.

With a deep breath, he let the reins loose and grabbed

the saddle horn. He was tempted to let his feet out of the stirrups but couldn't remember what Jackson or Mitchell had said about that, so he kept them right where they were. Mimicking Sonny's yipping at the herd, he tried yelling encouragement to keep the steers moving. He still felt self-conscious about calling to the cattle, and the tremor in his voice gave away what he was feeling. He couldn't help it; he was scared.

Halfway across, Bannon heard a yell racing across the water. A big cottonwood tree trunk was hurtling through the current and aimed at the herd line! Nobody was close to it. Jackson turned his horse around and swam back, but he couldn't move fast enough. His horse didn't much like the idea of turning around in the first place and fought him most of the way.

The dead tree slammed right into the middle of the strung-out herd. And everything changed. Every steer in the water stopped what it was supposed to be doing and began to mill around in midstream, all trying to deal with this strange thing that had come crashing into them. The more they milled, the more riled they were becoming. Bannon had never seen anything like it!

Riders on each side were yelling and trying to ride into this wild mess. Checker managed to separate four from the edge and get them headed toward the far bank again. Sonny gave it a chin-out try that ended with him clinging to his horse's neck with his derby gone and his nose bleeding all over his shirt.

Then Tex's horse got a headful of the crazies and lunged sideways in fear. In the next instant, handsome Tex disappeared into the gray water. He came up a few seconds later, gasping like a newborn baby. Then he started slapping the water with his hands and screaming like it was the end of the world. Elias Harrelson, big-bellied and with arms to match, pulled Tex to the far bank. Elias was laughing all the while, in spite of the seriousness of the moment.

Reilman tossed a long loop at the centermost steer, but

could only catch a single horn, not enough to hold it. Finally, he let the rope loose and gave the noose a quick flick up and off the horn. He tried again, but nothing better came of it. Now it was getting too risky to throw into that bawling mess: a man and his horse might get pulled under. Stopping this cattle swirling would be difficult and dangerous now. The steers were crazy with fear.

Four different riders tried to get to the center. Checker, Woodman, and two others. But there was no way to get through that many steers swimming around, wide-eyed, banging into each other and making things worse. Pushing from the outside would just make it a circle of death. None would allow themselves to be separated from the others. Drowning was waiting any man or horse who got caught in the wrong place. Another rider was down. Woodman pulled Clanahan from the swirling water and toward the shoreline.

Senselessly agitated, the steers circled tighter and tighter. At the center were a few steers next to the tree trunk, bobbing up and down. Two steers went under. Then a third. None of the three came up.

Loss from drowning was going to be high unless a cowboy was lucky enough to break inside soon and get them headed for the far bank again. Mitchell and his big bay were now in the water, and he was yelling something from behind. Bannon couldn't tell what he was saying.

Bannon didn't remember making a decision to do it. Fact is, if he'd thought about it, he probably wouldn't have done it. Certainly, it wasn't the safest thing he'd ever done. But it was a lot safer than trying to ride into that mess of horns and shoulders. Bannon jumped off his swimming horse and onto the back of the nearest steer. Grabbing wet skin with his hands, he pulled himself on its broad back, lying flat against its body.

The steer didn't seem to mind. Of course, there wasn't much it could do, except try to swing around in the water or go under. Bannon wasn't waiting for it to figure that out. Bobbing alongside, right against his steer was another big one. Closer to the center where the log was.

Crawling off the first steer, he eased over onto the second steer. Pointed horns slashed back and forth, trying to catch its strange rider. But it couldn't buck in the water.

As soon as he regained his balance, Bannon left this steer, half-crawling, half-sliding onto a slightly smaller white animal. And then onto another one. He was nearing the middle now. If he could get to one more steer right in the center of the swirling, maybe he could convince the soaked and fearful animal to leave and the others would follow.

His long johns were heavy with water, making it harder to move his legs quickly. But the underwear's rough texture helped him stay on. He had no idea how long it took to get to the middle. As close together as the cattle were, it wasn't too hard to crawl from one to the other until he reached the dizzy center of the whole mess.

His concentration was fierce. He was the only man in the river. If he slid off now, he would drown under the cattle before anyone could get to him. But he wasn't going to fall off. He wasn't going to die. With a half inhalation for courage, he leapfrogged onto the back of a large steer, dark brown from the water and mean looking—and moving next to the log itself.

This would be the new leader! The steer just didn't know it yet. Bannon grabbed its white horns and directed the animal into a straight line toward the far bank. Every muscle in his arms were a lever against the steer's resistance. A huge head shook hard to get rid of this thing on its back. But Bannon wouldn't budge.

After a hesitation that seemed endless, the animal began swimming toward the beautiful northern shore as intently as if it never wanted to do anything else. Using his bare feet, the young cowboy pushed away first one milling steer that was in the way, then another, and another, to open the path as best he could.

Gradually, the rest of the herd began to follow Bannon and the big steer out of the death circle. Behind him, he could hear Sonny and Jackson whooping, followed by other yells of encouragement. He was riding high and fancy.

Suddenly, a bump from behind threw him off balance and he slid into the water, like a wet otter on a slippery bank. As he grabbed like crazy for something to hold onto, the big steer continued toward the far shore, oblivious to the loss of its driver. It didn't even look back.

Thrashing about, trying to keep his head out of the water, Bannon felt a hand grab his arm and pull him slowly above the water. It was Jackson. With another lift and a little scrambling, the young cowboy was behind him on his horse. Bannon wasn't sure, but he thought Jackson said, "Amen."

Hearty greetings and nodding heads met them as they slopped up the far bank and onto dry land. The cattle were streaming across smoothly once more and being guided toward a flat open meadow and into a huge, gentling circle to graze. John Checker was holding Bannon's horse, its head down and dripping wet. Bannon slid off Jackson's horse and took the reins.

Checker smiled and said, "Well done, cowboy."

That made it all worthwhile. Bannon stood there, dripping wet, not knowing what to say. "Thanks, I . . . thanks," he mumbled. Checker gave him a hearty pat on the shoulder and jumped back on his own horse.

Clanahan rode close and said, "Sure and you must be Irish to do a fine thing like that. Your mither herself would be proud today."

Other riders were passing, leaning over to give him a pat on the shoulder and to tell him how good he'd done. Captain trotted over, stood at his feet, and barked joyously, as if in tribute. Then the ugly dog shook its body furiously, sending sprays of water in all directions, especially on Bannon.

Pete Foster loped up, his face like a racoon who'd found the mother lode of food, and hollered, "Hot damn, Bannon! You sure nuff showed us what a man kin do when he puts his mind to it. That's the tough way to git a shirt clean."

Soaked completely, a shiver shot through his back in spite of the hot dry air. He wasn't sure why. Just cold water probably. Looking up, he saw Dan Mitchell, grinning as wide as the river.

"That thar's a trick not for the meek," he said, loud enough for others to hear. "You'll do to ride the river with, Ty Bannon. You sure will."

Before long the herd was on the move again. Nobody even tried to put clothes back on, riding in wet long johns, boots, and hats. To Bannon, it was a grandly silly-looking sight: grown men working hard in their underwear. Like craftsmen, the crew even-spaced the animals, not allowing them to bunch up, especially at the rear. Overheating from crowding came easily. The herd's movement forward was little more than controlled grazing. Bannon couldn't have cared if it had been straight up the side of a mountain; he was higher than the red hawk circling overhead. The four miles to the evening's bedground went by before he realized it.

As soon as the chuck wagon rolled in, Tug began work on dinner. It was closing in on five o'clock. He would have a hungry bunch on his hands tonight. Fear mixed with hard work made any man hungry. To give them something different, he decided to roll the beefsteak in flour before frying it. Most of the men liked the taste.

Instead of beans, he would fix what he called "spotted pup." Pete Foster had another name for it. The dish was rice with raisins, apple slices, and brown sugar. The farm boy loved it and Tug decided the dish was to be served in his honor tonight.

"Hey, Tug! When's chuck? I could grab a steer and swallow it whole!" Tex yelled as he walked into camp from the remuda.

"Glory be, if'n the good lad ain't right!" Clanahan hollered cheerily from his squatting position beside the newly started campfire. Other cowboys loudly added their thoughts on the matter.

"Hold yer hosses, you riverheads! I'll tell ya when the vittles is ready! I can't cook an' drive a wagon too!" Tug growled back.

That was enough to redirect the drovers' attention to rehashing the river crossing, followed by more backslapping for a red-faced Bannon.

"Tug, I'll ride out and take a look for grub for ya."

The feisty cook looked up and was surprised to see Henry Seals, fully clothed, with a cigarette dangling from his snarled mouth. It had to be the first time the surly cowboy had volunteered for anything. In spite of Seals's sudden generosity, Tug wasn't excited about giving him the responsibility to ride out in search of additional food. He preferred to bestow the honor on his favorites, Tyrel Bannon and Sonny Jones.

But he hadn't planned on asking either of them—or any of the hands for that matter—to go out after the day they'd had. Everywhere he looked, tired men were trying to dry out long johns, boots, and gear. He also didn't think this part of the trail was inhabited by anyone. Still, it never hurt to try.

Tug licked a spoon, plastered with biscuit dough, to momentarily give him time to consider the request. Then he shrugged his shoulders, nodded approval, and sent Seals on his way with a wave of the utensil. In minutes, the cowboy was gone from camp and the feisty cook thought no more about it. Maybe he had misjudged the cowboy.

As soon as the bedground was out of sight, Seals spurred his horse hard and broke into a run. He rode in a north-westerly direction, racing the mount full out for nearly an hour. The land wasn't as flat as it appeared, accented frequently with low hills and shallow arroyos that slowed the horse's pace, in spite of his constant spurring.

But he knew where he was going and took every possible shortcut, following a stream for a quarter mile, then leaping it at the narrowest point and heading due north through a maze of cottonwoods. Thin shards of late-afternoon light cut through the trees as he cross-whipped the horse with his reins. His heart was in his throat, pounding. He didn't notice the steady stream of grasshoppers, butterflies, and birds fleeing in front of his thundering disturbance.

As he rounded a small hill near his destination, a turkey scattered in front of his horse. Seals jerked the reins hard in surprise at the loud, methodical flapping. He was sweating; his mouth open and dry. Regaining his poise, he stopped the lathered animal completely and dismounted.

Twenty feet ahead was a lone cottonwood tree standing sentinel over a scum-covered pond. Under the tree was a man and a horse. From the looks of the area, he had been there for at least two weeks. A lean-to was barely visible, its position concealed within a wedge in the shallow bluff cradling the north side of the pond. This was one of three checkpoints used by the McCallister gang, part of their systematic approach to rustling Texas trail herds.

"You sure as hell took your time gettin' here, Seals," growled the big-shouldered man, with an oversized mustache and matching wiry eyebrows. "I was beginnin' to figger you got found out and they hanged your ass."

Squatting beside the pond, the square-jawed man made no effort to stand while Seals dismounted and walked toward him. Under the man's long, once-white coat was a double-rowed bullet belt carrying two holstered pistols; the left one with the butt forward. At his side, a Winchester lay on the bank.

Beneath the gnarled tree was a cold fire, placed there to filter smoke from signaling his presence. Saddlebags and a bedroll were inside the lean-to. Two dead turkeys lay beside a black skillet and a blacker coffeepot. Neither had been dressed. Remains of a third turkey rested on a spit of branches over the fire.

Scattered about the ground were splatters of beans, peach juice, and opened cans that once held both. A half-empty whiskey bottle was propped against the tree trunk. Another bottle, completely empty, was lying at the pond's edge with brackish water seeping into its open top.

"Can't exactly stroll out for a picnic, Iron. I'm supposed to be lookin' for a ranch or whatever we might buy some food off'n. Seen any out this way?"

"How 'bout some Comanche wickiups? Will that do?" the man answered sarcastically, relighting a half-smoked cigar. His jaw was testimony to days without shaving. Signs of past meals were tatooed on his shirt, pants, and coat.

Seals looked down before getting into the speech that he'd been rehearsing since first spurring his horse. He inhaled to chase away the jitters and started talking much too fast.

"Tell Star that I don't like the looks of this one." Seals paused and waited for some reaction.

Iron-Head Ed said nothing, chewing on the end of the cigar like it was candy. Both men knew well the two primary rules: never more than two herds were taken a season, and none from ranchers well known in Dodge. Star McCallister also insisted his men leave Indian weapons behind when they attacked, so Indians would be blamed. That way the local law never got excited, if they even heard about it. Since the vast majority of herds were getting through without trouble, as far as Dodge City was concerned, there was no rustling problem. That's exactly how

Star wanted it. The strategy was simple but effective, controlled but lucrative.

He had seen his father take brazenly foolish chances, practically daring anyone to do something about his behavior. Ultimately someone had. The son was not going to make the same mistake.

Everything was measured and secretive. No matter how easy the rustling had gone, greed would not push him into stealing more herds than planned. Rather than the law, he feared arousing the force of angered Texas cowboys combining to take justice in their own hands.

Star McCallister had grown up in his father's saloon, observing more evil things than any youngster should. His mother turned into an alcoholic prostitute, leaving him to his father's rough guidance. But even at an early age, he did not consider himself cut from the same cloth as his father. He knew of J. D.'s other children, even if his father never admitted fatherhood of John and Amelia Checker.

At the age of 24, he bought one of Dodge's better saloons from a man who was selling to move to St. Louis. No one in town knew the former owner never actually made it to his next destination. After intercepting him on the trail, Star killed the unsuspecting man and took back his money.

Star McCallister worked hard at making himself well liked by the marshal and his men. Food, drink, and women were always available to them at no cost. The same was true for selective town leaders. His base well in place, he turned carefully to the creation of a masterful rustling operation, one that was making him very rich—and soon, very powerful.

But everything depended upon execution. Swift, deadly execution. And that was the third rule: the gang would attack with overwhelming force when the drovers least expected it. Usually a day or two out of Dodge City. It was Seals's job to tell the gang when the best time was, to slip in liquor to lessen the drovers' alertness, to get the herd's papers, and to cut loose the remuda when the attack came so it would be difficult for survivors to follow the raiders.

All of it would happen lightning fast, ambushing the cowboys while they slept and running off the cattle in the night. By the time any of the trail herders arrived in Dodge to report the theft, the herd was long gone and there was nothing to be done. The proper papers would have been presented to the buyer with the McCallister insider delivering the herd as the foreman. The money would be moved quickly into bank accounts in other towns.

Taking a deep breath, Seals continued, "When I got hired on the Triple C . . . didn't know John Checker would be ridin' with 'em."

"Who the hell is John Checker?" Iron asked.

"If you was in Texas you wouldn't ask that! John Checker used to be a Texas Ranger. A damn tough one."

"Used to be?"

"Yeah, he quit—and joined this drive after we were on the way. Must've been a month in, I reckon." Seals was feeling better now, his nerves were under control. "I didn't even know who he was for a few days."

"So . . . what are you sayin'?"

Seals was exasperated. Iron-Head Ed wasn't pretending, he just wasn't smart.

"I'm saying . . . tell Star that I think we shouldn't try to steal this herd . . . We should leave it alone and take the other one instead."

"Well, Star sure as hell ain't gonna hit Shanghai's herd." Iron spoke with the cigar in his mouth, his breath a fiery mixture of whiskey and strong tobacco that repulsed Seals, but he tried not to show it.

"I know that, dammit. But Harry's with a herd from Valverde . . . and Whitey's supposed to have one comin' behind me . . . from somewhere! Let's take those two instead."

"Well, Star ain't gonna like this one bit, Seals," the square-jawed man said, scratching his chest through his dirty shirt. "I saw him walkin' around wavin' your telegram and saying how easy this one was gonna be. This here Triple C ain't never been to Dodge before. He was real happy with your choosin'."

"I know that, Iron."

"Well, he'll ask, dammit. Do you know where the trail boss keeps the papers?"

"Yeah. Yeah. In a metal box . . . in the chuck. Won't be no problem gettin' that at the right time. It's Checker I'm worried about."

"Maybe you oughta shoot him."

"Maybe you oughta stick your head up a buffalo's ass and whistle too," Seals spat in exasperation. "I wasn't hired to kill nobody. An' I sure wasn't hired to go up against John Checker."

"Well, all right, I'll take your report to Star. Damn! See you at the shack."

Seals nodded. He stood slope-shouldered with his hip shoved to the right, trying to think of something else to say to help Iron make Star McCallister understand the trouble they would face if the gang tried to rustle the Triple C herd. Nothing new came to mind, so he repeated his concerns, much to Iron's obvious dislike.

Then with deliberation, the sarcastic cowboy went through the litany of detail that Star would expect to hear about the way the herd was being handled. When Seals was finished, Iron pushed out his lips in a silent whistle and ran his tongue over his sun-blistered mouth before speaking.

"I dunno why he makes us go to all this trouble an' sneakin' around. Why can't we jes' take whatever herd is close? There's always one comin'. Kinda like brown water," Iron said, grinning and displaying marred and broken teeth, obviously proud of his analogy.

"So we don't git a whole bunch of Texas cowboys comin' after us, stupid."

Iron-Head Ed frowned. Seals was instantly alarmed that he had overstepped his play. Iron may be slow but he was no man to ridicule.

"Think Star'll know this—what's his name?"

"Checker. John Checker," Seals repeated patiently, relieved that Iron wasn't focusing on his earlier statement. "Oh, I doubt it. Don't think the boss has ever been to Texas. But you can tell him the man's as good as Clay Allison."

"I reckon you're afraid of this Checker, Seals."

"Yeah . . . if you had a . . . ," Seals caught his words, "if you were up against him, maybe you could handle him. Not me."

Iron beamed at the compliment.

"I'm gonna take one of them turkeys, Iron," he said walking toward the campfire. It was time to return to camp.

"What fer?"

"So it looks like I did something besides windy with you."

CHAPTER 4

BEHIND THEM WERE the North Canadian, Canadian, Washita, and the Red rivers. Unlike the Wichita, these crossings had been fairly easy, although bank-full. Near the northern bank of the Canadian, they had ridden past three fresh graves with handmade crosses.

Now they were well into the Indian Nations. The Western Trail, and the Triple C herd's course, lay straight through this untamed country. Endless plains were laced with tall grass, dense woodlands, and wandering buffalo. This was home to the civilized tribes of the Cherokee, Creek, Choctaw, Chickasaw, and Seminole.

Occasionally, a tribe's representatives would formally present themselves to the crossing Texas herds, demanding a tariff for passing through the Nations. Nonpayment usually resulted in Indian trouble the rest of the way. None had presented themselves to the Triple-C so far.

Far worse than blackmail were the wild bands of Comanche and Kiowa roaming the rolling hills, waiting for unsuspecting passersby. Checker and Sonny had chased away eight Kiowa warriors early yesterday, killing three. The Indians were hiding, waiting to ambush riders as they passed. Tug kept one of their lances in the chuck wagon as a souvenir.

"Them Kiowas be singing some death songs in their lodges tonight, Bannon," Pete Foster growled and spat. "Yessirree. Bad choice for them redskins to run into. Checker and Sonny."

Water had been the bigger problem, or the lack of it. Canteens now held little more than a few brackish swallows, and these were sipped preciously. Watering holes were merely tantalizing mud, used up by the herds passing in front of them. But the shortage of water was about to change. Ahead of the herd was blackening sky.

Bannon rode half-asleep. He didn't notice that for an hour they had been riding toward a horizon filling with huge patches of darkness. Others were already wearing their oilcloth slickers. For him, though, a sweet dream of a naked, black-haired woman making love to him still lingered and distracted him. That was the nice part of his early morning, the lady in the dream.

The bad part was the result of that imagined passion: the discovery of stickiness around his groin as he lay wrapped in his blankets. Wiping himself with a wet kerchief and slipping on his pants, all while remaining blanketed, had been awkward but necessary. Otherwise he would have been the laughingstock of the camp. Jake Woodman, sleeping next to him, had been preoccupied with his morning ritual of massaging his feet. For that distraction, the young rider was most grateful.

Bannon finally looked up at the horizon. Maybe it was time for him to wear his slicker. Reaching back, he unloosened the saddle tie strings around the rolled-up slicker and shook it open.

His gray horse flipped its ears back as the long coat was unfolded, but didn't find the noise objectionable. Bannon sighed thankfully. He had been warned that some of the half-broke animals would become frightened when a slicker suddenly loomed behind them, a yellow ghost making strange noises. Bucking and running usually followed, anything to escape the perils of this strange yellow beast. Bannon didn't want the embarrassment or the likelihood of being thrown. "Thanks, hoss," he said, petting the animal on the neck in gratitude after his coat was on and buttoned.

Light rain was dancing on his shoulders. But a hundred yards away was a sheer wall of water! Nowhere was there a place to hide from the advancing blackness. The herd was disappearing into it like animals entering another world. Jackson came galloping back from his swing position.

"Tyrel, this is gonna be a mean one," he counseled, worry cutting into his mellow voice. "Herd will try to turn on us. Run, maybe. If there's lightning, get rid of your gun. Canteen. Spurs. Anything metal. Do it fast. We'll come back for 'em. Whatever you do, don't let steers on both sides of you!"

Before the young rider could respond, Jackson had wheeled his horse and was returning to the heart of the storm. Two days before, the farm boy had learned Jackson's father had been a slave who bought freedom for himself, his wife, and his baby son. The black man, with his eyes filling, related how high his father valued being able to read. He made certain his son could, even though the elder Jackson could not. Jackson was about the same age as Bannon was when his father died.

Bannon liked the way Jackson spoke so proudly of his late father. It helped the young rider put words around his own clouded feelings about his father's premature death: a loss that had created terrible hardship and emptiness for his family.

Like the riders and steers before him, Bannon rode into the wall of driving rain. He couldn't see anyone or anything ahead or behind. One minute he was getting sprinkled on; the next, he entered a waterfall.

"Man alive," he said out loud, "this gives me the shivers!" His horse flinched as if in response, lowered its head, and walked on. Bannon's whole body was beaten down into a soggy mess. The exposed bottoms of his chaps were giant brown washrags; his hat was pulled down around his ears: a black, unshaped mess on his shoulder-length light hair. Pounding rain was a Gattling gun against his slicker. He hunched his shoulders, trying to hide within himself.

Blurred shadows flickering through pounding sheets of

water were the only signs that a herd existed. A streak of lightning illuminated the horizon. Its twin sank light deep into the same ground a half mile away. He rode on. Unthinking. His head lowered against the gale. But suddenly he felt that something was wrong!

Blinking his eyes to clear them, he realized his first impression was right. The herd was turning. Every steer, every cow, was turning around and going back. They were turning their tails to the storm and heading back. Ahead men were shouting, barely heard above the rush of water. Here and there a pistol shot rang out. Another lightning bolt dwarfed the gunshots.

The herd was running! Stampede! Stampede!

Suddenly, Checker and Mitchell raced toward Bannon. Waving coiled lariats, they were headed for the new front of the herd, once the drag. Mitchell swung wide as Checker pulled alongside Bannon. His eyes were bullets beneath his sopping-wet Stetson.

"Follow us, Ty," Checker yelled over the roar of the storm. "If we can get in front, we can slow 'em!"

Like a ghost, the ranger was gone. Bannon reined his reluctant gray, turning in the direction of the vanishing point rider. His right boot slipped out of the iron stirrup and he lost his balance. Seizing the pommel, his arm strength kept him from falling. After two strides, he was in control again, both feet secure. In two more strides, the gray was running full out, trying to outrun the storm. Lightning turned golden the far side of the herd. Crazed steers thundered mindlessly into the day-turned-night.

Bannon charged past a chain of longhorns. Out of the blackness came the flash of a sharp horn, grazing his gray. Luckily, the contact was slight, drawing a ribbon of blood along its chest. The mustang jerked sideways and ran even faster, as crazed now as the steers it pursued. Bannon leaned low, extending toward the animal's outstretched neck. He couldn't stop the horse if his life depended on it.

Ahead were the bobbing silhouettes of Mitchell and Checker. The front of the herd was a hundred yards farther. Lightning struck into the middle of the herd itself. The smell of sulphur and burning flesh cut through even the thick wall of rain. Between the bellowing, thunder, and the roar of the rain itself, Bannon strained to hear the two leaders' commands. They were trying to gather enough men to turn the herd. Were they getting close to an arroyo that curved eastward? He vaguely remembered passing it. Yes, they must be close. That would be the place to turn them. Pistol shots rang out as advance riders fired in front of the animals to scare them into obeying.

Bannon eased his horse away from the steers; several were swerving toward them. Or was it his imagination? He couldn't tell what the ground was like; had they already passed the arroyo? His only reference was the herd itself and he was flying past cattle like they were grazing. His nerves were jammed against his skin; at any moment, he and his horse could hit a hole and go flying.

Behind him there was a scream! A scream that rammed itself into his already fearful mind. Impulsively, he glanced backward but saw nothing. Turning around he saw a huge outcropping of rock looming in front of him. Too late! His horse reacted with a huge leap to clear the corner entrance to the arroyo. He grabbed the pommel with both hands, his reins flew, his heart jumped. For a breath, he thought the cinch would snap with his off-balance weight pulling against the saddle. His arms strained to hold him in place; his legs squeezed the flying horse.

The gray's jump was not enough, landing midway up the incline. It struggled to get to the top of the slippery rock pile. The gray made a second savage lunge and scrambled for the safety of the ridge's crest.

"Come on, hoss! Come on!" he screamed above the roar of cattle and rain.

They were on top! Standing alone on a finger of land

little wider than the horse. The rock-lined outlet connected with the wider plains, hiding the long, winding gulch below. With neither rein in his hands, he was lucky the mustang didn't run farther. Instead, the exhausted horse stood and shook itself fiercely, letting the closeness to death rush through its own body and out into the black. Bannon held the pommel, both fists turning white; his teeth rattled and his own fear was jarred loose.

Behind him, the sky was softening; the storm would soon be reduced to a straggling regiment of scattered raindrops. The herd was matching the slackening rain, slowing itself gradually into a walk, many in the cradle of the arroyo but many spread all over the soaked plains.

Into the arroyo's shallow river galloped a riderless horse. A bay. Whose was it? Bannon remembered Jackson was riding a sorrel. Recovering his reins, he nudged the horse back down the incline. It was time to return to their earlier objective.

Running wasn't a natural thing for cattle. They had played themselves out, storm or no storm. Like a brown army, the longhorns in the arroyo slowly turned; some were again walking north to Dodge as if the storm had never happened.

He hadn't been there to help. The echo of insecurity passed through him. What would Mitchell and Checker say? What would they think?

After four tentative steps, he knew the gray's right foreleg was hurt. Dismounting reluctantly, he kneeled beside its leg. Nothing he could see was wrong. But when he held the lower calf, the animal winced and withdrew the hurt limb. Bannon shrugged his shoulders, glanced up at the clearing sky. He would walk.

Jake Woodman approached, grim-eyed and gloomy-faced.

"You all right, cowboy?" he asked, riding next to the ridge as Bannon led his horse down the unsteady rock. His fallen hat was waiting on some mesquite. The storm had left behind its meanness with lots of mud, slippery rocks, and small ponds. Yellow streaks across the dull gray sky signaled what everyone already knew: the storm was over. A narrow stream meandered down the center of the arroyo bed. Steers were splashing over the sodden ground, pounding it into a slick mire.

"Yeah, but my hoss is lame. Ran right into it."

"We sure rode through purgatory and back, didn't we? Bet we lost a hundred head. Damn!" the methodical cowboy continued, water dripping from his soggy hat. "Reilman's not far behind. Worst part's over. We'll get 'em moving north again. Unless they're too damn scattered," he reported without changing his expression. "Pete's hurt. Webster's down. May be bad."

Bannon thought the controlled point rider was going to say something about his feet but must have realized how it would sound. Especially after talking about two fellow riders being hurt. The point rider loped on, more terse than usual. Several other drovers passed, each man pausing to check on him. Since the Wichita crossing, he was one of them. Only Seals had continued his hazing; if anything, it had become more personal.

Bannon walked his limping horse, splattered with mud, toward a makeshift corral Reilman had thrown together. It was backed up against a solitary grove of cottonwoods. The wrangler was hard at it, roping new horses for just about everyone. As he walked, Bannon enjoyed the show: Reilman could make a lariat snap in the air like a blacksnake whip or lay it as soft as a snowflake over a horse's neck without the animal even realizing what had happened.

Next to the remuda was the chuck wagon. A small fire was snapping and popping and coffee was bubbling in a huge black pot. Tug always kept wood and dried buffalo chips on the rawhide apron underneath the chuck wagon.

Tug called that apron a "possum belly." Just in case it was needed. Like now, when there wasn't a dry piece of wood within twenty miles. Twenty feet farther west, Dan Mitchell and Stuart Willis were replacing a back wheel on the calf wagon.

Tug was hustling to put together something hot for the crew to eat. Working alone like this was singing in church for him. Good chuck was coming, whether they were ready or not. Tug didn't care a hoot about the fact there was water everywhere a fellow looked. His task was to ready a hot meal for a worn-out trail crew. They ate on the run. This driving day was shaping up to end well after slap-dark.

Pete Foster was sitting on a log next to the cooking fire. Every breath brought sharp pain from the grizzled cowboy's chest. Tug had wrapped Foster tightly with a ripped piece of blanket but it didn't seem to help. The horse had been shot; a broken leg left no choice.

Blowing the steam off a cup of coffee, the old cowboy was saying to Tug, "Them underworld ghosts just opened up the land and grabbed my pony. Goddamn craziest thing you've ever seen."

Both men laughed until it hurt the injured man.

"Now, don't let the boss go dealing me out of this game, Tug," he added. "Ol' Foster here still got plenty of chips."

A few feet away lay an unconscious Jacob Webster; his head was bandaged with traces of old blood lining his face. Bannon remembered Webster was riding a bay, the one that was running free in the arroyo.

Clanahan, Wonson, Seals, and Harrelson were waiting for new mounts as the young rider approached. Elias Harrelson was complaining about his boils. He'd put a chaw of tobacco on them before breaking camp. The burly man was the only one without a slicker. His constant blue suit coat was soaked and looking more disheveled than usual. Each man was inside himself, not even "talkin' hoss." Fatigue was in reddened eyes and weary stances.

Seals saw the advancing Bannon, said something to the

others, and yelled, "Where you been hidin', greenhorn? Lightning scare you up your asshole?"

There was light laughter. Bannon didn't respond. He led his worn-out mustang to Reilman and told him what had happened. While the young rider unsaddled, the salty wrangler examined the leg.

"Bruise is all, Ty. Be ready to run again in a few days. Tough little hoss," Reilman stood. "How 'bout that little bay o' yurn, ya haven't used it fer a piece."

"That'd be great."

"Be 'bout four damn hosses down the line," the wrangler said, leading the gray away to the corral.

Working fast, Reilman handed off a sturdy brown to Wonson, followed by a short-legged black to Clanahan and a quiet bay to Harrelson. Sonny Jones rode up to change horses, as did John Checker. A few minutes later came Tex, not looking as dapper as usual; his water-soaked hat was flopping around his ears.

Henry Seals's eyes sparkled with the new audience. Reilman handed him his next horse, but he would bully the farm boy some more before moving on. Strutting toward Bannon as he received the black, Seals glanced around to see if his audience was watching. The young rider's back was to Seals as he cinched up.

"What're you doin' to them cows that makes 'em run away, boy?"

"Goddammit, Seals, leave him alone. Bannon's more of a goddamn cowman than you'll ever be," Randy Reilman snapped over his shoulder as he stalked a husky bay for Sonny.

Seals was silent for a moment, as if evaluating the reason for Reilman's remark, then returned to his prey. He stepped closer to Bannon as he gave his cinch a last check to make sure it wasn't too tight. Jackson had told Bannon right off that it was hard on a trail horse to have its belly strapped hard.

"What's that nigger friend o' yours been teaching ya,

boy? Hell, he probably don't even know who his papa was."
Seals's ridicule sent a shiver through the young rider. And
something deep inside exploded.

Bannon's response was silent and without thought: He
spun on his heels and slammed a right fist deep into Seals's
stomach. A left jab followed in less than an eye blink into
the same unprotected area. No discussion. No threats. It
was the last thing the bully expected.

Seals was bigger than Bannon, three inches taller and at
least thirty pounds heavier. But the blows were delivered
with all of the farm boy's considerable upper body
strength reinforced by the hot fire of resentment too long
held. Seals's recent meal flew out in direct response to the
intense pain, splattering all over his boots. He doubled
over to give relief to his screaming stomach.

But Bannon had just started. A right uppercut, thrown
from his toes, caught Seals's exposed chin full force and
sent him flying backward. Bright with intensity, Bannon
ran over to the flattened man and pointed his finger at
Seals's pain-twisted face.

"Get up, Seals. Get up! I've taken all the words from you
I'm gonna take. Now you're gonna eat every single one of
them. Get up!"

Seals stood slowly; a thin line of blood wiggled down the
side of his chin from his split lip. He took a long breath,
grabbing air. Ignoring Bannon's challenge, he took two
slow steps toward his fallen hat, laying three feet from the
waiting farm boy. Seals leaned over slowly and picked it
up. Rising, he tossed the hat toward Bannon's face and
followed with a vicious right-hand haymaker aimed at the
same point.

Bannon was expecting it. He ducked the flying hat with
the turn of his head and stopped Seals's blow with his left
forearm, forcing it up and away.

Seals's trailing left hand was a hair slow to cover the
young rider's right fist as Bannon followed the cowboy's

missed swing with a short jab to Seals's open chin. It would've stopped a steer. His head snapped backward like it was hinged. Seals's arms flailed wildly as he lost control.

Bannon grabbed the falling cowboy's shirt and wouldn't let him stumble to the ground. Holding the wobbly cowboy with his left hand, Bannon's right fist punched over and over into the fear inside of Seals. Finally, he let the sullen cowboy collapse into a cross-legged position like an old Indian; his head laying against his chest.

From behind Bannon, John Checker put both hands on the young man's heaving shoulders. The move was firm but not restricting. With the first touch, Bannon spun around, ready to continue the battle with whoever was there. His mind and body were locked into a fighting frenzy. When he saw who it was, he stopped. Puzzled but ready. If the former ranger wanted some, bring it on.

"That's enough, Ty. We need what's left of him." Checker spoke with a quiet authority.

"I'm through. Unless he says something else I don't like," Bannon snapped, looking straight into the ranger's hard face. "Then you'll have to stop me too. Tell Seals to keep his mouth shut or I'll shut it again. I've had enough of his crap."

Checker was surprised at the command but indicated his agreement with a silent nod and a slight grin.

From behind them came a challenge from Sonny, "Don't even think about it, Seals."

When Bannon spun around, Seals was still sitting, but with his hand on his pistol. Sonny Jones was standing ten feet away with his right hand next to the pistol at his hip, coiled for Seals's next movement. There was nothing happy in his usual joyful face. He looked like a man ready to kill.

Seals was no fool; shooting at Bannon's back was one thing, facing the likes of Sonny was another. He lifted his gunhand up and away from the weapon in a real exaggerated motion. The young rider looked at Sonny and nodded his thanks. Turning back around, Bannon saw Checker returning his own pistol to its holster; the young rider hadn't seen the first movement at all.

Moments later, Bannon rode away. There was nothing to stay around for. A day's ride was going to be crammed into an afternoon and early evening. His point had been made clearly. Now it was time to work. As he cantered into position and the fury of the fight evaporated, his mind began chewing on his insecurity. Mitchell would probably fire him. Fighting among drovers wasn't tolerated. It couldn't be. The job was too tough to worry about feuds and the like.

He should have been able to keep his anger in check, no matter what Seals said or did. His growing remorse was about letting the trail boss down, not about beating Seals. He remembered the time after a similar fight with a neighboring farmer who tried to steal a milking cow.

"Tyrel Bannon, you should be ashamed of yourself," his mother had said. "A man who can't keep his temper isn't a man. He's an animal." She wouldn't listen to his explanation.

Sonny Jones was singing a song about the fight as he rode up. It snapped Bannon out of his reverie. The tune was to "Camptown Ladies" with words about Bannon smashing Seals into the ground:

"*Ty-rel Ban-non . . . bust his head. Pound him. Pound him.*"

Turning around in the saddle, the young rider shook his head, contradiction in his unmarked face. Kicking up chunks of mud, Jackson came alongside the young rider, passing Sonny at a gallop, but swinging wide so he wouldn't disturb the cowboy's horse.

"I just saw Seals," Jackson said, his voice edged with concern.

"I don't give a damn about Seals."

"I know that. Man, do I know that! I hear you damn

near tore him in two," Jackson continued. "I thank you for stepping up for me. No man's ever done that, white or black. I am in your debt, Tyrel Bannon."

Worry creasing his brow, he paused before going on, "But I'm not talkin' about fisticuffs. I'm talkin' guns. He'll try to kill you. When the trail's done. Maybe before. But I'll be watching him, Tyrel. He's got to go through me first."

Bannon answered with a bucketload of confidence, more than he felt. But the young rider knew his friend was right. Seals would seek revenge. Somehow. And Bannon was pretty sure it wouldn't be in a straightforward fistfight. The man was a bully, working with a big mouth and not much else. Now that the man knew Bannon saw him that way, words wouldn't work. Would Seals resort to using a gun?

Jackson galloped ahead to take his position at the swing. His fresh roan mustang moved smoothly at his touch.

Opening and closing his fists rapidly, Bannon studied his sore knuckles. Be lucky if they didn't swell up. Seals's jaw had taken a price, although it was well worth it. His fight would be the talk of the camp for a day or two, but he was hoping it would be forgotten soon after that. Maybe he should talk with Seals. No, that wouldn't work. The cowboy was never alone and would not take well to any peace talk in front of the others. Best to forget it. When Seals's face was healed, the matter would disappear along with it, he reasoned to himself.

Three steers made a foolish judgment to curl off into a patch of mesquite off the trail, and that ended his introspection. Twenty yards farther ahead, a cow and her calf meandered away from the flow of the herd. He spurred the bay to meet the interruptions.

The horse was hungry for it and quickly cut all five of them off from further travel indiscretion. Bannon patted the high-strung animal alongside the neck. He hadn't used the small bay in three days. Not one of his favorites. Had a tendency to spook quicker than the rest of his string. Still, it was a great day for an eighteen-year-old cowboy to be alive and on the trail.

In spite of cracked ribs, crusty Pete Foster loped up on his way to a swing spot. He reined in beside Bannon. Whiskey was strong on his breath.

"Goddamn, boy, I ain't seed nuthin' like that whippin'! Whoo-ee! You sure found out Seals was all gurgle n' no guts. Glad yer on our side, Ty Bannon."

He didn't wait for any words from the young rider, easing ahead immediately to his place. Most men would be lying hurt for a week after being thrown like he was. Bannon didn't blame him one bit for the "medicine."

A fifty yards away from the herd, the chuck wagon rumbled along. Looking over, Bannon saw Tug waving at him to come over. The bald cook had filled a bucket with cold saltwater for Bannon to soak his hands. It was sitting inside the closed wagon tongue so the young rider could stick his sore knuckles in the bucket without anybody knowing what was going on. Looked like Tug had asked for help with something. The cold saltwater would keep the swelling down.

When he rode off, Tug gave him a great big grin and said, "Seals had it coming, boy, and you brought it wrapped with ribbons."

That set off a snicker, then a chortle that rippled along his belly, gaining momentum. Then it erupted into loud laughing and snorting. He was laughing so hard Bannon thought the little man was going to fall down. Tears drained down his cheeks and his belly shook like an upset cat was under his shirt.

Sundown came and darkness followed, and they were still in the saddle. It was late before they settled the herd for the night. The bedground was soggy but flat, easier on cattle than on men. A string of cottonwoods stood solemnly on the west edge. A swollen stream ran along the east. Tired animals would go nowhere tonight, a small consolation for worn-out punchers.

Foster was already asleep, eased into it by more whiskey. He wasn't the only one; half the drovers were settling in for the night. Unless they had guard duty. Six were sitting around the small campfire, yarning. Jacob Webster hadn't regained consciousness and was kept in the chuck wagon. Mitchell and Tug had made a pallet for him. Campfire talk said Webster was dying.

Henry Seals wasn't in good shape either, but he only felt like he was going to die. Bannon's battering had turned his face into a purple pumpkin, his stomach into a painful plank. Two teeth were broken and he had a cracked rib. His movements were measured and his talking, throaty.

The drive had lost at least a day in its quest to reach Dodge. But Mitchell was more concerned about the condition of the beef than the calendar. He wouldn't push the herd far tomorrow; no man would complain about that.

After supper in the dark except for a lantern and the campfire, Bannon was sitting with Jackson. Both were squat-legged on the damp ground, sipping coffee, twenty feet from the fire and the men there.

"Lordy, Tyrel," Jackson said, breaking the silence, "that was more water than we saw at any river so far. Makes me think of ol' Noah and his big ark boat—you know, that story in the Holy Bible. 'On that day all the fountains of the great deep burst forth, and the windows of the heavens opened. And the rain fell upon the earth forty days and forty nights.' "

Bannon chuckled at the recital. The young rider tested his cup's contents. To blow on the surface was his decision.

"Watch them beeves tomorrow, Tyrel. Likely to be grouchy. We'll be lucky if a horse doesn't get cut."

Bannon sipped his coffee carefully. Jackson wasn't waiting for a reaction.

"Mitchell says we're only going to move 'em eight miles. A nice flat piece yonder." Jackson pointed northeast.

"Mind if I join you, boys?" John Checker stepped out of the dark and stood next to them.

"No, not at all. We'd like the company," Jackson replied. Bannon nodded his assent.

He sat beside them on the ground and took a long pull on his cigarette. His movements were catlike, even when relaxed. Bannon was unsure of what to say, so he blurted out that the sunset had been pretty. Checker agreed and squashed the burned-up cigarette in the ground.

"Bannon, you shape up like a bad man." Checker's words cut through the evening's dampness and through the nervousness Bannon felt with him sitting near. He added, "No offense."

"None taken."

Bannon was proud that he hadn't stuttered. Being called a "bad man" was a compliment, at least to the young rider. It meant "a bad man to give any trouble to."

Checker continued, asking about Bannon's handling of a gun, a pistol in particular. A little surprised, the farm boy said he was better with a rifle but that he could generally hit what he aimed at. With anything. Apologizing for getting personal, Checker asked if he'd ever shot a man or been in a gunfight.

"No. Just food for Ma's table. An' Tug's," Bannon replied, his face giving the answer before his words. He was uneasy about where this was leading to. Maybe he should tell him about his older brother killed in the Great War.

"Bannon, I've been around guns . . . too much," Checker said. "Maybe that's why . . . anyhow, don't worry about Seals comin' up behind you. I'll be watching. And he knows it."

Yellow streaks from the campfire made warpaint over the ranger's chiseled cheeks and mustache.

Bannon replied confidently, "I appreciate that. But I reckon it's my fight."

"When you and Seals are facing each other, it will be. Not before."

"I can handle it myself. Seals should let it lie."

Jackson interrupted, "Checker, this boy had every right in this fine world to knock the hell out of that bastard. Seals more than had it coming."

"No argument there. Seals definitely had it coming. In spades," Checker agreed, his eyes meeting the black man's in understanding.

"The way I see it, Seals's pride is hurt. You beat him bad, Ty," the ranger said to Bannon. "He's not a tough man. Now he knows you know it. An' the rest of us, too."

Jackson spoke again, "That fight should have been mine. Seals said some things about me that he shouldn't have. I reckon the next time he faces me. My gun."

"No," the young man insisted. "If that fool wants to pull leather with me, tell him to have at it."

Trying to defuse the subject, Jackson took a different approach. "I'm surprised Dan took him on. Had his reasons, I guess. Not much there to like in the man."

Setting his cup down, Bannon surprised even himself with his continued hard response. "Don't know 'bout that. But I don't take to being pushed none. Back home, folks'd be almighty wide-eyed to hear I took so long to tear into him."

"Wouldn't doubt it, Tyrel," Checker said. "But if it comes to guns, you stay calm. Getting mad means making mistakes. Block out everything else. No different than the hunting you do."

Checker took out the makings, sprinkled tobacco into the paper, and rolled a cigarette. Orange flame from his match was trailed by white smoke wandering away from his mouth. The white trail of smoke curled around his chiseled face before seeking the dark sky.

His talking made Bannon wonder just what he'd gotten himself into. His sudden silence only made it worse. But Checker changed subjects as abruptly as he had jumped into the first one.

"What are your plans, Ty . . . after the drive?"

"Well"—the young rider's eyes brightened as he answered—"I'd sure like a ridin' job with the Triple C."

"Have you talked to Dan about it?" Checker asked, taking another drag.

"No. No, not yet," Bannon was uncertain of the ground he was on, "Didn't figure I'd be too high on Mister Mitchell's list—after this morning."

Checker smiled; it was a warm and friendly smile. Bannon was beginning to like this man.

"I wouldn't worry about that," he said reassuringly. "If you'd like me to, I'll put in a word with him."

"Thanks! That would be swell!"

Changing the subject again, the ranger indicated things might get dangerous after they cross the Cimarron and slid into Kansas. In the past year, two trail herds had been rustled and both crews killed, supposedly by renegade Sioux.

"You figure it's rustlers?" Jackson asked, hunching his shoulders to ease the growing stiffness in the cooling air.

"Yeah, I do," Checker answered. Then he quickly asked, "You don't have a rifle, do you, Tyrel?"

"Got one at home," he responded defensively, realizing the moment it was said how immature his words sounded.

Jackson told a story about an Indian fight they had run into on a drive five years ago. As he spoke, Checker pulled his pistol from its holster and checked the loads. A reflex or a nightly ritual, Bannon wondered.

The young rider noticed all six chambers were filled. Most cowhands kept the one under the hammer empty; his was. That way the gun couldn't go off when it was pulled and hurt the cowboy. Checker was sure enough of his handling that he didn't want his firepower cut down. The former ranger stood, said he needed to get some sleep, and walked away. His exit was decisive but not rude. Bannon watched him go and decided to add a sixth cartridge to his own pistol before going to sleep that night.

CHAPTER 5

"TYREL. WAKE UP, Ty."

It was John Checker, his rugged face barely visible in the night's heavy shadows. Bannon shot upright in his blankets. Where was he? Hadn't he already done his turn at nighthawk? What night was this? Darkness lay about the camp. No signs of dawn anywhere.

The young rider's blinking eyes focused first on Tug, working near the chuck wagon, a lantern turning him into a study in yellow. Then, he slowly looked up at the former ranger standing over him. Sleep was draining from his face and alertness coming.

"Kiowas ran off twenty horses. About an hour ago. You, me, and Sonny are going after them. Now," Checker reported in a low voice, sipping coffee as he spoke. "Tug's got us something to eat. On the way. I think we can catch up quick if we're at it. Reilman's saddling your horse."

That was it. Checker turned away and headed for the chuck wagon and more coffee. In the shadows, Bannon could see the foreman moving toward Checker. They spoke for a few moments before both headed for Tug, who had become the center of activity.

As the young rider's head was clearing away the wisps of the night's dreaming, he reached for his shirt and pants and slipped into them. But none of the buttons on his Levi's fly ever seemed to want to go into their holes when he was in a hurry. Finally the buttons slipped into place and he took a deep breath as if something significant had been accomplished. The farm boy turned to his boots and shook them to make certain no creatures had found an interesting stopover for the night. His spurs jingled lightly in the darkness as he stomped the boots in place. The moment was always special to him, like a badge of manhood.

A wave of his old rumpled hat did little to restore it to any shape. Laying the forlorn thing on his head, he pulled it in place with a hard tug of the brim, letting the tie-down thongs flap against his cheeks.

Kneeling, he rolled his blankets tightly and tied the bundle with a piggin string. Somehow, the blankets now looked like they belonged out here, instead of on a bed at home. He stood and grabbed the roll by its tie. The roll would be tossed into the chuck wagon, with the other gear, when he went for something to eat. Almost forgetting, he leaned over and reached for his pistol belt and the heavy Walker Colt.

Now they were nearly across the Nations. Less than a week from the Cimarron River and into Kansas. The land had changed somewhat since the North Canadian, becoming harsher, with long stretches of clay, buffalo grass, and scrub oak.

This was wild land, where many outlaw gangs retreated after raids in Kansas and Missouri. Bands of Kiowas and Comanches crisscrossed in stark contrast to the civilized tribes of Cherokees, Creeks, Seminoles, Choctaws, and Chickasaws. Tahlequah, capitol of the Cherokee nation, was a few days' ride away, but no other town or even a ranch was within a four-day reach.

Water had again become their biggest problem. What few watering places they came to had already been used up by the herds in front of them. Yesterday morning, Reilman and Woodman had dug a hole in a spongy bottomland that had once held water and raised enough to give the horses a reasonable watering. The cattle had left before they started digging. The men rode unwashed and changed horses four times a day to keep from wearing them down.

Jackson had told Bannon that a small pebble in his mouth would cut the thirst. The young rider decided if one was good three would be better, so he rode with his mouth full of three stones. He wasn't certain it helped but didn't want to tell his friend that.

The herd itself was beginning to move continuously toward the distant Cimarron, never bedding down. Their black tongues hung low from open mouths as they bawled night and day. Some of the animals had gone temporarily blind from lack of water. They would recover, Jackson told the young rider. In the meantime, he should watch out because they could bump into a man's horse. More coyotes sneaked around the outskirts of camp than ever before. Their howling didn't keep many from sleeping, though; everyone was too tired.

Jake Woodman was scheduled to search for water this morning, hoping to find something between here and the Cimarron. To make matters worse, Indians had been spotted numerous times, but none had come close since Checker and Sonny had driven them off. Now they had struck swiftly. The young rider shivered when he realized how close the red savages had been to the camp. He wondered how Checker knew it was Kiowas, and not Comanches or some other tribe.

With a forced wink, Tug handed Bannon a hot biscuit with two fat strips of bacon lying over it, "Grab yourself some Arbuckles, boy. Ridin' hard on a empty belly ain't good for a growin' boy."

Jackson brought Bannon's fast-running black horse. Bannon was surprised to see him up but learned from Tug that the foreman had asked the black cowboy to take the point with him while Checker and Woodman were gone. Bannon immediately noticed a rifle scabbard had been added to his own saddle. In it was Mitchell's Winchester.

"The boss figured you might have more need of it than he will," Jackson said, answering the unspoken question.

Sonny appeared from the dark, leading his horse, a long-legged dun, his fastest. Sleep was slow in leaving his face. It made Bannon feel better, knowing he wasn't the only one struggling to wake up. Sonny nodded a greeting, smiled, and broke into a hoarse rendition of a few lines from "The Old Chisholm Trail."

Sonny slapped Bannon on the shoulder and sought some coffee. Off to the side Checker was talking quietly with Mitchell. Tug was working at the hinged tabletop that came down from the back, where he usually was before mealtime. With practiced skill, he pulled one thing after another from its place in the honeycomb of drawers and cubbyholes above the table. Finished, he brought saddle-bags filled with food and handed it to the young rider. He gave Sonny two boxes of bullets as well.

"You got enough grub for one good day. Canteens are filled. Took most of our barrel water, so don't waste it," the feisty cook growled.

As they swung into the saddle, Mitchell walked over to Bannon. He patted the young rider on the leg and said, "Checker asked for you when he discovered the loss. That's a high compliment, boy. Ride well."

Minutes later, they rode north out of camp. It was too dark to see much of anything except dark shapes. As they moved, Checker shared the story of what had happened. Indians had hit the remuda silently on the far north side about an hour or so ago. Tex, the remuda night guard, had fallen asleep in the saddle. (Mitchell had been posting guards on the horses since they hit the Nations.) It had probably saved his life. Checker thought it was Kiowas by the shape of the moccasin tracks.

Even though it was husky dark, Checker had no trouble following the stolen horses. To their right, morning streaks were signaling daylight was on its way. They rode silently, each man into himself. Checker smoked a cigarette; Sonny chewed on a big wad of tobacco; Bannon finished a second biscuit. They rode fast, taking advantage of the marked passage in the dry dirt. A smooth gallop took them through a spongy bottomland bristling with tall, morning-wet grass, past a line of cottonwood surrounding a dry pond, through a fat thicket of blackjack, then out onto an open prairie.

The main herd would move ahead without them. Checker had told Mitchell it should take no more than a day, coming and going, for them to recover the horses and catch up with the herd. The Indians didn't have much of a lead. Most likely, the Indians were starving. If they had come in and asked openly, Mitchell would have cut out three or four head of steers as a gift. But horses were too precious to lose. And twenty head missing meant the remaining string would have to be worked even harder. Some men would be walking into Dodge if the trio didn't get them back.

The sun was high overhead before they stopped under a lone cottonwood standing beside what had once been a creek. A half mile away where the creek bed turned and headed north, a jutted rock passage was the prelude to a wooded valley. Checker motioned for Sonny and Bannon to dismount.

Shadows from the ridge covered them as the beef jerky, hard biscuits, and canteens were passed. The pause would be for minutes only, long enough to give their horses a blow and for the riders to shove food in their mouths. They stood and held the reins, allowing their horses to graze.

"Remember that old owlhoot . . . Mysterious Miller?" Sonny asked the former ranger as they ate. "The one that was always changing the way he dressed?"

"Yeah, he was a piece of work, wasn't he," Checker said with a grin. "He should have been an actor or something—instead of robbing banks."

"Woulda been a good one, I'll bet."

Bannon wondered where the two had met but didn't ask. He wolfed the piece of beef jerky, then downed the last of a biscuit with a long pull on his canteen. He watched Checker pull his Winchester from its scabbard, lever it, and ease the trigger down to an uncocked position.

"I think we're close," Checker said, swinging into the saddle again. "Unless I miss my guess, they're holed up on the edge of the woods. Just over the ridge. Couldn't be more than a few hundred yards."

"You figure they've seen us?" Sonny asked.

"Don't see how they could miss us."

"I was afraid you were going to say that," Sonny said, then took a swig from his canteen and yanked his rifle from its scabbard.

Bannon was the last to check his gun, savoring the weight and balance of the trail boss's Model 1873 Winchester. What a fine weapon, he thought, holding the reins in his left hand as his free hand slid along the cold metal.

Sonny looked at him, "Don't know what we might be facing. Those bastards might have already left. They couldn't outrun us with all those horses. They might be waiting. If there's firing, don't hesitate. Shoot to kill."

After the other two were mounted, Checker directed them to split up so that each man would clear the ridge at a different point. Sonny rode north fifty yards and Bannon went the other direction the same distance. They would climb the ridge onto the open flat ground at the same time. Once there, the woods itself was no more than two hundred yards away. That's where Checker thought the Indians and the Triple C horses were. It was just a hunch, but he knew they couldn't be much farther ahead and there weren't any signs of dust anywhere.

The young rider couldn't get rid of the nervous tension that grabbed at his breath and made it jagged. He kicked the black forward and soon was climbing the side of the ridge. Holding the Winchester in a ready position was awkward as he kept the horse cutting back and forth up the rock-strewn incline. His eyes worked the top of the ridge as it came closer. Beads of sweat rambled down his face and stopped long enough to burn his eyes.

As he cleared a rock-edged ravine, shots tore into the day. Sonny's climb was stopped by the firing; his horse jerked and spun down into the arroyo. Checker yanked his horse to the left and down the embankment toward Sonny. Bannon was instantly alone on the top of the ridge.

Instinct directed his rifle. Everything was in slow motion. Eight warriors on painted war ponies rode screaming at him from their position near where Sonny had disappeared. Holding the reins in one hand, he fired again and again. Bullets whizzed past him, their heat unnoticed by the young rider as he entered a battle trance.

One warrior flew from his mount and crumbled into the flatland's dust. Another slumped against his horse's neck. Suddenly from the far left came Checker, now on top of the ridge, followed by Sonny on foot. They had caught the Kiowas in a crossfire almost as quickly as the war party had hit them. Two more warriors exploded from their mounts and hit the ground like crushed flowers.

Bannon drew his heavy Colt as the remaining four warriors approached. The Winchester was empty. Acrid gun smoke tore at his nostrils. He cocked the pistol and aimed at the closest brave, but there was no need. Without a sound, they broke from the charge and galloped toward a distant horizon. Sonny fired his Winchester twice more. The young rider just watched them.

Bannon holstered his pistol and began jamming new loads into the Winchester's side-loading mechanism. His eyes jumped from bullet to vanishing warriors and back again as he did.

His horse was standing still; Bannon looked down at the reins in his tight left fist, only then realizing he had halted the animal. The attack was like a bad dream. It didn't seem real at all, more like a swirling wind that passed through and left everything changed behind it. Remembering his horse, he glanced down and around at the animal's heaving body. No signs of injury. He patted the black on the side of the head and said, "Good job, Blackie, good job."

Checker rode slowly toward him; Sonny followed, bow-legged. Their smoking rifles pointed toward the sky. Both were more shadow than feature with the afternoon sun at their backs. Off to his right, Bannon could see movement within the darkness of the woods. He squinted. The Triple C horses were grazing quietly there.

"You all right?" Checker asked.

"Think so," Bannon said.

"Good. Let's round up the ponies and head back. We'll need to rope one for Jones here. The dun went down . . . for good."

The young rider glanced at Sonny, his face was more distinct now. A frown covered the cowboy's forehead.

"Sorry," Bannon said quietly. "That was a good hoss."

"Yeah. Sure was. Never gave me one day of trouble."

A queasy feeling came over Bannon as the reality of shooting a man sunk into his mind. He had killed another human, maybe two. He wondered if Checker or Sonny felt this way. Down in his stomach was a churning that wouldn't stop. Not that he had any choice about the killing. It was shoot or die. Yes, he'd do it again if he had to. Maybe that was what the churning was all about. He glanced back at the brown bodies.

Checker eased his horse beside the young rider and pulled out a bag of Bull Durham. Creasing the selected paper, he sprinkled tobacco across the seam, licked, and sealed the smoke. A match snapped off his belt buckle brought the cigarette to life. Only then, did he speak.

"You had no choice, Tyrel. If they had their way, your scalp would be swinging on a lance tonight," Checker said softly. "They'll come back for the bodies. Usually they take them. No time, this time."

Tyrel looked at the ranger's face and knew Checker understood what he was struggling with inside. Just that awareness made him feel better.

"Come on, Tyrel, let's find one for Sonny," Checker said as he cantered away toward the herd.

The afternoon sun was already hot on his shoulders as Henry Seals rode slowly toward the cabin. He had told the other drag riders that he was going to make a wide swing to pick up strays. No one questioned his leaving. That was over an hour ago.

Down through an arroyo he eased his sweating horse. As he recalled, this was the only way into the hideout area from the south. It had been a year since he had last been here, but everything seemed familiar. Late afternoon shadows within the ravine were twisted and angry. Minutes later, he rose out of a deep cut that served as a spoon into another stretch of heavy woods. Out of habit, he reined in to listen and look back. Nothing.

Ahead was a run-down sod cabin and a small stable, slipshod structures built years earlier by the elder McCallister. Strings of smoke from its chimney were caught in the blue sky. A bay horse stood quietly in one of the stalls. Seals rolled his tongue across his lips; whoever was inside would have seen him by now. Maybe Iron-Head would have some food ready. Or a drink. Seals hoped so; his belly was growling.

"Hey, the cabin! It's me, Seals!" he yelled from fifty yards out, his hands still held away from his sides just in case Iron or whoever from the gang was waiting was feeling a little jumpy. No one answered.

"Hey, inside! I'm hungry and thirsty . . . hope you got something to chow on!"

Astride his horse, he sat unmoving, twenty feet from the planked door with the leather-strap hinges.

"Get in here, Seals!" said Star McCallister. Seals wasn't expecting the boss. He was instantly on alert and hurriedly swung down.

Inside the log-lined cabin, a fire glowed bronze in a blackened and cracked stone fireplace. Windows were closed with wooden shutters, each with a crossbar for support and small holes for looking and shooting. Only one large room, it usually reeked of fried food, urine, and sweat. But now the pungent aroma of beef stew filled every corner.

Setting on the fire's edge was a coffeepot and a large black crock of stew. A bedroll lay on the packed clay floor. In a far corner was a permanent stack of Winchesters.

At a long, gray table sat a short, thin-faced man. Star McCallister had already brushed the trail dust from his gray business suit with matching vest and silk cravat. A pearl-handled revolver in a shoulder holster was barely visible under his coat. A gold chain with a dangling fob crossed his vest. Soft kid boots were adorned with stylish silver spurs. His frail physical appearance and fine clothing hid a cruel, shrewd mind.

McCallister's bowler hat was pushed back on a pale forehead, showing curly blond hair and a clean-shaven, youngish face with light blue eyes set too close to a small, sculptured nose. Occasionally, his eyelids would flutter like a hummingbird in pursuit of nectar. It was something he didn't have any control over.

"Boss . . . I-I-I wasn't expectin' you. Thought Iron—"

"My god, man! What happened to you?"

Seals had forgotten how his face must look, still carrying the yellowing bruises under his right eye and across his nose from the fight with Tyrel Bannon.

"Ah . . . got kicked by one of the hosses."

"Damn! That must've hurt. Get yourself a plate of stew, Henry," McCallister said warmly. "Iron made it today, before he left. Quite good, I'd say. After you've eaten, we'll talk."

Seals wasn't certain how to react. Instead of his boss being angry with him, McCallister was actually quite friendly. The surly cowboy let the smell of food push his concerns aside, at least for the moment. He picked up an iron plate and a big spoon from a lopsided counter against the wall and headed for the fireplace, holding the plate with both hands to hide his nervous twitches.

Watching the cowboy lift the steaming stew onto his plate, the businessman took a cigar from his inside coat pocket, bit off the end, and snapped a match to life on the rough-edged table. White curls of smoke soon floated lazily above him. Seals sat down with a heaped plate and ravenously attacked it.

McCallister rose and went to the window, slid away the crossbar, and opened the wooden shutters. He stared outside, silent and apparently lost in thought. Seals concentrated on the meal, which was equal to his boss's description. He would compliment the meal when finished.

As Seals sopped up the last trace of gravy with his forefinger, Star McCallister turned from the window. From his vest pocket, he removed the gold watch attached to the chain. A metallic click preceded the opening of the lid. McCallister checked the time and returned the watch to its pocket. He looked up as if it were the second to become fierce. His hot stare pierced Seals's composure, unsettling the swallowed stew.

"Iron tells me you think we should leave the Triple C alone," McCallister stated, his eyes capturing Seals's paling face.

Seals gulped and nodded. There were no words close to forming in his mind. He hid his hands beneath the table so McCallister couldn't see them tremble.

"A former ranger is with the herd. Is that correct?" McCallister continued methodically. He walked toward Seals, stopping at a cupboard with one door barely hanging in place. From it, he took a half-filled bottle of whiskey. He began searching for glasses and found two cups. He poured several fingers into both and handed one to Seals. The surly cowboy knew the rules about drinking on the job. His hand was quivering as he accepted the cup.

"Go ahead, Seals. It's all right. This time. You need it."

Seals gulped down most of the cup and found his voice. "Yes, boss. John Checker. He's a known man . . . in some parts of Texas."

"Don't worry about this Checker. First thing, Waco will blow him apart with a buffalo gun. Then we'll open up on the others."

"But what if . . ."

McCallister's thin fist slammed against the table and Seals's eyes widened. The businessman snarled and replied in a reedy voice, "I said, don't worry about it. Or do you want Waco to know you don't think he's good enough?"

Seals knew he shouldn't press the situation further. Besides, Waco was the best man with a gun he'd ever seen. Waco would kill the former ranger from long distance before Checker could get in the way, and that was that. He shivered at the thought of Waco demanding to know if Seals had doubts about the gunman's skill. His eyes blinked away the fear and he glanced up at McCallister, hoping his boss hadn't seen the reaction.

Without apparently catching the shiver or pausing for any response from Seals, McCallister was already outlining what was expected of his spy. The attack would come when the herd reached a bedding ground close to Dodge. Seals would point out Checker after camp was made. Waco would watch with field glasses from a safe distance. Touching the former ranger on the shoulder would identify him to Waco.

"He ain't easy to miss, Star. Tall. Hard-lookin'. Wears an

Indian war shirt kinda thing. And a fancy gun too. Black handles with some funny-lookin' circles on 'em. Foster told me it was Indian sign but . . ."

"Fine, that makes it even easier. You just walk up to him and lay a hand on his shoulder . . ."

"W-W-What should I say? He ain't much for jawbonin'."

"Thank him for being with the drive. Tell him you rode a lot easier, knowing he was there," McCallister answered impatiently. "Can you handle that?"

Seals was expected to ride out to get whiskey from one of the hidden gang when the camp was settled for the night. Upon returning, he would distribute it to his fellow drovers. He was also to steal the metal box containing the herd's papers from the chuck wagon. It shouldn't be difficult. After Tug was through with the supper cleanup, he usually sat around the campfire.

Leaving his horse saddled, he would return to the remuda and wait for Waco's shot to kill Checker. McCallister's men would then fire on the sleeping camp. Besides Checker, the nighthawks would be cut down by assigned shooters. As soon as the firing began, Seals was to cut the ropes, freeing the horses and get them running with him away from camp.

McCallister advised him to ride south before swinging wide and heading for the MC ranch. The gang would use their standard "evidence" approach: wearing moccasins and riding unshod horses, so all traces would indicate an Indian raid. Kiowa and Comanche weapons would be scattered after the attack was over. The stampeding herd would be brought under control later; other gang members would be waiting to turn them.

Seals knew the system by heart; they had used it every time so far, but still he listened quietly, knowing McCallister liked to repeat such details. A stray question wandered through his mind: which of the Triple C men he had ridden with wouldn't live to see Dodge? Besides Checker. He liked the idea of looking down upon the lifeless Tyrel Bannon. The miserable farm boy would rue the day he messed with Seals.

"Boss, what if Waco misses?" Seals said, finding enough courage to face his boss's reprisal and bring up the ranger again.

"Have you ever seen Waco miss?" McCallister responded with a smirk, chuckling at his own question, "Checker will never know what hit him. You just make damn certain your jobs get done. Waco will handle his end."

Then he said something that would puzzle Seals all the way back to camp.

"Hell, John Checker probably should have been riding with us from the beginning," McCallister spoke softly, almost talking to himself. He realized what he was saying and glared at the confused Seals. His eyes blunted with hatred, McCallister said, "Now get out of here and don't mess up."

Late afternoon on the trail, the men were bringing their thirst-crazed animals, in an orderly manner, to a spring-fed pond. Woodman had found it a mile off the established path toward Kansas. It didn't look like any of the herds in front of them had discovered this small oasis, either. The cattle were eased forward in groups; the rest were held far enough away so the animals couldn't smell the water until time to bring up another group.

The relay worked for a while. Then a thousand steers sensed the presence of water and exploded toward it. Six steers were trampled in the melee. In minutes, the pond was nothing more than a muddy ditch. Tex's good bay horse broke a leg and had to be shot when a blind steer rammed it. Tex was winded but unhurt.

John Checker, Tyrel Bannon, Sonny Jones—and Henry Seals—arrived at about the same time. Red streaks were tearing into the late afternoon sky. Too late to help turn the rush for water. But four riders wouldn't have made any difference; the herd was without reason. The horses Checker and the others returned to the remuda helped relieve some of the crew's frustration. No one noticed Seals had returned without finding any strays.

About half the herd had tasted the pond's rewards; the rest bawled their despair. The crew pushed them on to the Cimarron, and by the time they hit the river, at least two thousand steers were blind from lack of water. The herd broke for the water a half mile out and hit it running. But the Cimarron was low and the crossing was easy.

After guzzling the coolness, some steers sought the soft mud of the bank and horned into the waxy earth; some sank themselves into the water like bathers in the spring; others curved their tails and jumped about like young calves. None were as happy as the men. That night Dan Mitchell broke out a bottle of whiskey, and everyone celebrated the crossing and the return of the horses.

They moved smoothly into Kansas and much of the difficulty of the drive seemed to vanish. Even the land seemed more friendly. The prairie was a boundless bowl of waving grass, flush with game. The trail itself was seventy feet wide in some places. Burrowed fences paralleled much of their pathway; deep lines cut in the ground by plows. Kansas law said they were to be treated just like fences. Farmers did this to warn trail herds not to trespass on their ground. Dan Mitchell said to the men he expected them to respect their wishes.

Finally, the herd came to rest in a flat green meadow, half-surrounded by trees and a fine stream. The railhead at Dodge City was a day of easy herding away. Mitchell wanted to fatten the herd on this rich stand of buffalo grass before making the final push, so he decided to hold them here for two days.

The Triple C hadn't been there before—they had always used Ellsworth as a selling destination. But this boomtown was closer. Jackson told the young rider that Mitchell was eager to make a good impression with a fat herd.

No drover objected to letting the herd stay where they were and not have to ride the next day. Spending time out of the saddle, taking a bath in the stream, even getting in an afternoon nap sounded like heaven. To make things even better, Jacob Webster was up and walking. It made everyone brighten to see him on the mend. Only Seals seemed uneasy; he rode out early for his nighthawk shift, something he never did.

For the first time on the drive, Tyrel Bannon felt relaxed. His sunburned face was scrubbed clean before supper; his freshly washed, long blond hair waved softly in the early evening breeze. Even the additional freckles on his nose were tolerated by the young rider. A fresh shirt, kerchief, and pants—creek-washed and prairie-wind dried—made him smile all over.

Of course, the men were eager to celebrate the joys of a real town, too. After dinner, around the campfire, stories of what some figured to do in town became more fanciful as the night grew. Three hands—Tex, Clanahan, and Harrelson—had savored the pleasures of Dodge City before and were eager to share their experiences.

Bannon was very curious about what Dodge City must be like. Jackson, who had also been there, began describing the raw trailhead for the young rider—from the hustling business section of the city, to the growing residential areas, to the assemblage of every known civilized vice.

The young cowboy had never heard of so many different kinds of buildings and businesses being in one place. Mercantile establishments, trading companies, cafes, warehouses, shops, hardware stores, livery stables, general stores, tailor shops, all manner of business places, sprawling and spreading across the belly of windswept Kansas.

Tex interrupted, "Hell, boy, it's nothing less than the

wildest collection of drinking, gambling, dancing, and whoring that's ever been!"

Jackson quietly brought the discussion back to business, painting another picture of a sea of longhorns grazing along the winding Arkansas, outside of town, waiting for delivery details. Jackson's words made it sound like make-believe to Bannon, like some fairyland on the prairie.

"Tyrel, it's unbelievable," the black man said, puffing his pipe. "There'll be herds sold in Dodge that'll end up being delivered clear on the other side of Montana. Past the Yellowstone River, even. There'll be buyers that'll never see the cattle until they arrive."

"How does he know what he's buying?"

"Whatever a man describes, Tyrel, that's his word. His promise. A man's word is everything."

"Tyrel, you've never seen the like," Harrelson hollered over the campfire. "Hell, there's a whole goddamn street of saloons, gambling places, eatin' places, music halls . . . an' houses with sporting women who'll spin your ears off!"

Laughing at Harrelson's description, Tex flashed a face-wide smile and proudly proclaimed, "I'm gonna get my likeness done at that photography gallery place."

There was chatter about the big Opera House, Beatty and Kelley's Alhambra, Delmonico's Restaurant, Alamo, Comique, Lady Gay, and the Dodge House. Clanahan said the mayor owned the Alamo, so a fellow should be extra careful there. And the Long Branch, that was a fancy place for trail bosses, cattlemen, and beef buyers. Not ordinary drovers. It even had a five-piece orchestra and a billiard table!

"Now, Tyrel, me boy, you got to put your mind to where you are hurrahin'," Clanahan advised, with the orange stripes of the campfire turning his face into an Irish warrior's. "Glory be, if everything doesn't stop at the Deadline."

"What's that?"

"That, me boy, is the darlin' railroad track. They call it the Deadline, and a fine name it is," the Irishman said. "If ya be doin' wild things on the north side o' that track, your sweet self will be taken away by the fine constables there. An' you can swear on your mither's beloved soul, there's no love lost among 'em for Texas cowboys."

Jackson explained to Bannon that the south part of town was for the Texas cowboys and that the good part of town was on the north side, across the railroad tracks.

"Polite folks act like the South Side doesn't even exist," Jackson said. "It's quite an unusual arrangement, Tyrel, even for us Texans."

Everybody laughed. The three men estimated that there might be five hundred cowboys in town at any time. The number grew with each man's assessment. Standing most of the time to give his boils room to breathe, Harrelson said it was like "a great big party right in the middle of nowhere."

Most of the talk, of course, eventually centered on women. Bannon was kidded about being a virgin. Especially by Tex. The curly-headed cowboy loved telling yarns about bedding good-looking women everywhere he went. With his handsome face and fancy star chaps, it was easy for Bannon to see how Tex knew all the best women in Dodge City. Tex promised to take good care of the young cowboy.

Jackson eventually wandered off to bed; Bannon followed a few minutes later, leaving only the Dodge City veterans to banter into the night. Looking up at the star-spotted sky from his bedroll, Bannon thought about lying to the boys tomorrow and saying that he had done it with Mary Ross, a girl back home, so he could say he wasn't a virgin.

The two had enjoyed some good times out in the shed, kissing and touching. But he couldn't talk about any of that stuff, much less lie about it. Didn't seem right, even if they were only campfire windies. What if one of the crew ever met her? What if they told her outright what he had said? His loins stirred as he wondered what it would be like to bed a woman. Sounds like there's plenty of willing women in Dodge, he thought. *Maybe I'll go with Tex and find one when we get there.* Even in the dark his face burned with embarrassment.

Tonight and tomorrow night would be bittersweet for the young man, there was no way getting around it. His first real adventure was coming to an end. The day after tomorrow the herd would be sold at the Dodge City stockyards and that would be it. It was hard to believe the time had gone so fast. But the thought of returning home felt nice down inside. It would be good to see his mother again, to have her hug him and tell him how much he'd grown. Worry over him like he was some little child. At least for a day or two. Then it wouldn't be enough.

He didn't remember falling asleep. Toward morning something stirred him. Rolling over, he saw John Checker astride his black horse near the remuda. The camp was silent; the sky was an hour away from introducing morning. The former ranger was talking with Dan Mitchell. They shook hands and Checker left camp. The young rider wondered for a moment where he was headed, but sleep reclaimed his attention and he snuggled into his blankets.

CHAPTER 6

MORNING GLOW SETTLED on John Checker and warmed him as he rode toward his sister's homestead, the hand-drawn map etched in his mind. Amelia couldn't be more than three miles from the Triple C bedground. Almost due west. Inside, he was a boy once more, excited and apprehensive. Excited about seeing her; apprehensive about how she would receive him. He should have sent a letter saying he was coming. What if they had already moved? What if she was just being polite and really didn't want him to come? Questions hammered in rhythm to his trotting horse. Now that the reunion was so close, he was uneasy.

He pulled the small sack of tobacco and a cigarette paper from his shirt pocket and began to roll a smoke. After sprinkling tobacco along the creased paper, he returned the bag to his pocket, rolled the paper tight, licked the loose flap, and sealed it with his fingers. Checker placed the cigarette in his mouth and struck a match on the butt of his pistol.

The yellow glow was cupped in his hand, warming his rugged face. Smoke came out in a haze, then wandered skyward. The former ranger took off the flat-brimmed Stetson, wiped his brow with a shirtsleeve, and moved his head back and forth to relieve the stiffness in his neck. His long black hair resettled along his shoulders as he took another puff on the cigarette. He looked self-consciously at his gray linen shirt. This was the first time it had been worn, wrapped carefully in his gear until this morning. Just for this occasion.

When they parted this morning, Checker had told the

foreman that he would return to camp tomorrow, in time to help drive the herd into Dodge. Mitchell had grinned and told him that it wasn't necessary, "We can find our way now, John. You stay with your sister. I'll see you in town in a few days. I'll be thinkin' of you, my friend."

Seeking reassurance that they were still there, the former ranger touched his saddlebags containing gifts for Amelia and her family. The gifts had made the trip from Texas. He had meant to ask Jackson—and Mitchell—about his selections but had never gotten around to it. He had a leather-bound book of poetry for Amelia and some soft blue cloth for a dress, a tin of tobacco for her husband, a jackknife for young Johnny, and a cloth doll for Rebecca. Would Amelia or her husband not like his bringing a knife for their son? Maybe he should ask permission first.

None of the land was particularly familiar. It had been too long. He had ridden through this country briefly as part of a gang that operated from within the safety of the Nations, like many others. The owlhoot trail came five years after his mother died of whooping cough. They had lived in the rough buffalo hunter settlement that later became Dodge City. His mother had been a poor woman when she met J. D. McCallister, their father.

She fell in love with him. Two children were born of their union: John and Amelia. But J. D. McCallister never married her and refused to recognize those children as his. One day, McCallister left her without so much as a "nice knowin' you." Checker realized his father was a merciless crook even back then. The McCallister saloon was the hangout for his gang of fierce ruffians, rumored to be thieves and murderers.

Checker's mother took in washing and worked as a cook, trying hard to keep her young family together. When he was fourteen and Amelia eight, their mother came down with whooping cough. She was soon bedfast; the growing sickness eating away her strong will to live and care for her children.

"Johnny, Amelia, I . . . I . . . am pr-proud . . . of you," she said from her bed, unable to raise her head from the sweat-soaked bed, unable to say more than a sentence before vicious pain ripped at her frame. No matter how much she wanted to, the illness was not going to let her live but a few moments longer.

The tall teenager held one white hand; his sister, the other. Their world was a tiny dingy room smelling of laundry, candles, and death. Their mother's tortured face was all that mattered to them.

"M-m-my dearests, I am s-s-sorry that I can't s-s-stay." The coughing took control. She tried to say "I love you," but the sickness would not give her that last wish as it devoured her last breath. John Checker and his sister stood beside her bed and cried, cried until there was nothing left inside their souls except the ache of her leaving.

After the simple funeral, Amelia was taken in by neighbors, but Checker would not be consoled. He found a knife, and with grief driving his anger, he ran for McCallister's saloon.

"Hey! What's this?! What are you doin' with that knife, boy?" a brutish, acne-scarred man asked as young John Checker entered the saloon, yellow from oily lamps and gray from layers of smoke. He was one of McCallisters's thugs, sitting at a table, drinking with three other armed men. J. D. McCallister was in one of the small back rooms with a whore. The scene was burned in Checker's memory, and it came alive again as he rode.

"Watch 'im, Lowell. I reckon that young sonovabitch is here to get at the boss," growled a tall, squinty-eyed man in a long buffalo coat. "That's his son by that Checker woman. You know, the one that jest died."

The distraught teenager, holding the sharp blade at his

side, walked past the table without pausing or answering. The scar-faced outlaw sprang from his chair, pulling his own huge skinning knife from its sheath at his belt. From the rear, he grabbed Checker hard by the shoulder, swinging his sparkling blade toward the boy's neck.

Young Checker yanked himself away from the man's grasp and broke the outlaw's knife blow with his forearm, slamming it against the man's wrist. Checker's own knife moved in eye-blink response. The blade disappeared into the man's stomach and came out crimson. Checker raced to the back and ran up the stairs as the wounded man collapsed.

Two bullets tore into the wall after Checker.

"Goddammit, you bastard! Come back here! You can't go thar, boy!" yelled the buffalo-coated outlaw, a smoking pistol in his hand. The other two men from the table surged past the yelling man and around the widening pool of blood encircling the downed outlaw. Ignoring his gurgling pleas for help, they bolted after the boy.

Before Checker could reach the room where McCallister was, another door suddenly opened and a half-dressed woman grabbed his arm. She pulled him inside and bolted the door.

The buffalo-coated outlaw banged on the door and said, "Open the goddamm door, Rosie, you bitch, or I'll—"

"You'll what? Shoot a woman?" the prostitute replied haughtily. "Open the door yourself. I've got a double-barreled shotgun aimed at anybody who steps inside."

"You're bluffing. That goddamn kid just killed Lowell. Cut him open."

"I saw it. He tried to kill the kid. Go away! Leave him alone. I mean it."

Muttering was laced with loud curses as the two men retreated. After a few minutes, the honey-haired stocky woman opened the thick door and peeked outside. Satisfied, she called to the bartender and asked him to come up. Then she locked the door again.

The bartender, a husky man with a cigar wedged into the corner of his wet mouth, joined them in her plain room.

"You're going to have to leave town, Johnny," the man said unemotionally, without removing the cigar.

"Go easy, William," the woman said, "he's just a boy."

"He came after the boss in his own saloon and killed Lowell! That ain't Sunday School stuff."

"You know damn well it was self-defense. I saw Lowell try to knife him."

"I know that, too, Rosie. That's why the law won't be calling, but J. D. McCallister'll come after the boy, son or not. He's got to leave town. Either that or die."

Checker had no notion of why the whore and the bartender intervened on his behalf and saved his life. They sneaked him out before the McCallister men could drag him off and kill him.

Word traveled throughout town by the next morning, as McCallister and his men searched for the boy. But they never found him.

Young John Checker hid in the back of a buggy driven by the prostitute. The buggy stopped in front of the cabin of Thomas and Henrietta Rice, the god-fearing couple who had taken in little Amelia. Checker climbed out. A shotgun was clearly visible beside the prostitute in the seat as she quietly drove the buggy back to town.

Dominated by religion, fear, and his wife, Thomas Rice told the boy in no uncertain terms that he must leave immediately. The stiff-faced farmer said loudly, "Johnny Checker, I am sorry but your wrath will bring the unholy and unwashed heathens upon this home."

Rice paused and took a deep breath, his courage expended. Then he said, "They'll kill you, boy. They'll kill you. An' they'll kill us too. Just for bein' Christian to ya. Your sister will be well cared for in a Christian home here. You understand, don't ya?"

The teenager nodded, his arms folded to hold in the emotions pounding within him. Awkwardly, with a stiff smile on his face, Rice motioned for the boy to follow him. Young John Checker complied in a daze as they walked around to the back of the house. A saddled horse was tied to a scrawny tree next to the small cabin. The muddy brown animal was old, its head inches from the ground, its back swayed from long use.

Mrs. Rice brought out a large sack filled with food and handed it to him. She turned away quickly without making eye contact. Thomas Rice gave him a silver dollar.

His sister came running out of the house, tears spreading across her milk-white face. "I-I-I want to go with you, Johnny!"

Trying to be stronger than he felt, the boy said, "You can't, sis. But I'll come back for you."

"Promise?"

"I'll come back."

"Say you promise."

"I promise."

He turned to leave, his stomach in a knot so tight he didn't think it would ever allow him to eat again.

"Wait, Johnny . . . please," Amelia said, her face wet with despair, her eyes bright with fear. "I want something . . . of yours. To hold. Please."

The young teenager half-turned, not knowing what to say or give her. He had nothing, except the knife in his belt. She grabbed at his shirt and yanked a button from it. He hugged her quickly, not allowing her emotions to keep him from what had to be done. He mounted the horse and rode off, not looking back.

He wouldn't allow himself to cry until the cabin was a speck behind him. Then his resolve broke and his wail was a wild animal's. He fell off the horse onto the ground. Sobbing. The old gelding nibbled on a strand of buffalo grass at Checker's shoulders. He didn't notice or care. The reins lay loose on the ground. He sobbed until there was nothing left in his soul. Only then did he remount and ride on, vowing never to cry or care about anyone again.

The next day the three McCallister men from the saloon were close on his trail. Expecting pursuit, he had hidden near the first watering hole, among a cluster of cottonwoods and downed timber. It would be a likely place for his pursuers to stop for the night. They did. In the darkness, he killed one of the sleeping outlaws with a rock to the head. That gave him a pistol, rifle, bullets, and a good horse. He left as silently as he had attacked. If the other two continued to follow him, he was never aware of it.

After he left Dodge City and his little sister, he drifted, trying to live any way he could. In Liberal. In Abilene. In Wichita. Cleaning stalls. Sweeping floors. Washing dishes. Breaking horses. Fistfighting for prize money. Working cattle. Using a gun. Five years went by and the bark grew hard on this young man. His fists were quick; his gun was quicker. A rancher hired him as a bodyguard, in spite of his young age.

Then he met Sam Lane, a squat outlaw with a voice like a rusty water pump, the result of a bullet to his windpipe. Sam Lane led an outlaw gang and took a liking to the young tough, and Checker became an outlaw too.

It was a strange time for him; his outlaw days did not last long. While riding back from robbing a train in Missouri, his first, a shiver went through him; his dead mother was talking to him.

"What's the matter with ya, Johnny?" Lane said in his hoarse voice, looking over at his fellow outlaw. "Ya look like ya seed a ghost."

They rode without talking for nearly a half hour before Checker answered.

"Sam . . . I'm gonna ride on," Checker finally responded. "Today. Somethin' I've got to do. No offense."

The outlaw leader was stunned into silence again. Only the soft pounding of hooves cluttered the air. None of the other five riders heard the conversation.

Since then, Checker had always been on the law's side, as a Texas Ranger. His reputation had quickly spread along the border. He was happier with himself, but there was a hole in his soul that wouldn't heal. When a letter from his sister unexpectedly arrived, it had driven right to that emptiness.

Down through an arroyo Checker eased the big horse. Minutes later, he rose out of the arroyo into another stretch of heavy woods. Amelia's map had noted both. There! There was the big tree with the two gnarled trunks. That was one of Amelia's landmarks.

He was no more than two miles from his past. Close enough to need reassurance before going on. He stopped the lightly sweating horse beside the strangely shaped tree. Dismounting, he wrapped the reins around a low branch. To his right were the remains of an old campfire.

His hat became a container for canteen water that his mustang gratefully accepted. After a swig from the canteen himself, he looked for a comfortable spot to rest for a few minutes. Soon, he was reading that letter one more time, searching for special things between each word. It had become a litany for his soul.

Remounting, he rode slowly into a lake of grama grass, waving halfway up a man's knee and going forever in all directions. He rode through it with a drover's appreciation for its richness. Suddenly he saw the homestead, setting alone in the corner of a long valley. Small but solidly built, the ends of rafter poles poked out from under a flat roof. Centered in the front yard, a snarled elm spread gentleness as far as the porch.

There was a barn, a poled corral filled with horses, and a stone house for storing butter and milk, just as Amelia had described. A well was set twenty feet from the front porch. Along the back edge of the yard, a shallow creek ran easy-like toward the south. To the west was a long field of rowed corn; a line of hedge trees had been planted to protect the crops. He couldn't remember ever seeing a more welcome sight.

As he neared, the door opened and a tall woman came out, beaming. She was graceful, even striking, in a beige dress covered by a working apron. Long brown hair bobbed at her shoulders; her delicate face, with a small, thin nose, contrasted to the hardiness of her frame. A freshness about her returned Checker to a fuzzy memory of their mother. Amelia's cheeks were faintly flushed; her blue eyes grew wide with excitement. He would have known her anywhere. And it was obvious that she knew who he was! His heart raced. Their eyes met in a way that melted away the years. He heard somewhere in his mind, "I'll come back. Say you promise. I promise."

Behind her came a taller man, lodgepole lean with reddish-blond hair, an unruly beard, and a nose like a bent stick. A worn pipe was attached to the corner of his mouth. Checker sensed a goodness in Orville Hedrickson and a quiet strength, but also a wariness of men with guns.

Slipping between the man and woman came an eight-year-old boy. He was waving and smiling. Checker exhaled. He was home. What a happy sight, he thought. This was what life was all about. A man could see himself here—a wife, children, and a home. He jumped off his horse and she gave him a big hug.

"I knew you'd come! I knew it! I've been feeling it for weeks now." She cried and laughed, tears streaming down her face and onto his shirt where they held each other. "Oh my god! Oh, Johnny! Oh Johnny! Let me look at you."

His own eyes overflowing with elation, Checker struggled to find the words that would match his intoxication, but less than that tumbled out. "Amelia. I can't believe it. You're all grown up. You're . . . beautiful. You look just like Mom."

Amelia stepped back and introduced her husband. Orville shook Checker's hand with vigor. When the tall Swede spoke, it was obvious where he had come from.

"Yah, and it's good to see you, John Checker. *Valkomen!* My Amelia, she's bin a-talkin' that you vould be comin'. Yah, for many days. I thought she was woman foolish, you know. We didn't hear from you . . . Yah, this is very good."

Finally, the former ranger leaned over to speak to the young boy. "How are you doing, son? You must be Johnny."

Young Johnny grinned widely, displaying two vacant spots in his teeth, and reached out a hand for him to shake. The boy's eyes rarely left the Colt on Checker's hip. He wanted to keep holding his uncle's hand as they walked toward the house, but dared not to. Instead, he walked as close to him as possible as the group headed toward the house.

Amelia was doing all the talking, exploding with the joy of her brother's unexpected return. Every third sentence was "I knew you were coming." It slipped through his mind that soon she would scold him for not writing. But the thought was quickly swallowed in his own swelling joy.

"Orville, take John's horse to the barn, will you, please, sweetheart?" she asked more efficiently than warmly.

"Oh, no need to do that, Amelia," Checker admonished, suddenly realizing how he had intruded on their lives. "He's never been in a barn. I'll take care of him in a minute or two."

Amelia didn't respond to his statement and continued giving orders, "Johnny, you help your father with your uncle's horse."

"Aw, Ma, I want to stay here."

"Your Uncle John will be here when you finish. We'll be in the house. You take care of his horse first."

Checker decided it would make no difference to protest further and said simply, "That's mighty nice of you. I'm sorry to be coming . . . unannounced and all but . . ."

"Don't be silly, John, we're just glad you're here . . . with us," the gentle-faced woman said. "I knew you wouldn't write. I just knew it." She squeezed his arm playfully.

Reluctantly, the boy went with his father to take the sweating horse to their barn while Checker and his sister went into the house. Without asking, she guided him toward the bedroom where Rebecca slept.

Checker followed with a lopsided, kidlike smile on his face as they looked in on the napping little girl. Then Amelia showed him around their home, and Checker felt more and more out of place. He was a man of the gun, and this was the home of a family, his sister's family. This home carried a man's strength, but it also held a woman's caring. Would he ever know such contentment?

Framed pictures of family atop a cabinet in the corner of the bedroom caught his eye. One was of Amelia's family, taken before Rebecca was born. Another was the same as in his pocket watch, only larger: a long-ago shadow of his mother, Amelia, and himself. He touched the glass and imagined how hard it must have been to come up with the money for these photographs. She watched him, silent for the first time since he had arrived. He turned toward her, pulling the watch from his pocket as he did. With a sad grin, Checker clicked open the lid and showed her what he had kept.

Without a word, she stepped to the cabinet and picked up two small items displayed among the photographs. A timble. A button.

"Remember these?" she asked, the corner of her eyes wet. "This was Mother's . . . and this . . ."

"Yeah, off my shirt," he said, smiling. Then he wiped

his finger across his nose and added, "I can't believe you kept it."

"That's all I had, Johnny. That . . . and your promise."

"I was mighty slow getting around to keeping it, wasn't I?"

"Your baby sister says yes. Your grown sister says you're here now—and that's what counts." She gave him a long hug.

They were silent, both staring at the photograph and the little keepsakes. Amelia stepped away, dabbing at her eyes with her apron.

"I've got work to do for dinner, John. Why don't you join the menfolk at the barn. We can talk more after we eat."

"I hope you're not going to any trouble for me, Amelia, I—"

"Hush, big brother. I'll do what I want." She smiled brightly and kissed him on the cheek.

He went outside and walked to the barn. Inside, he found the stall where his black horse stood. The big animal had been rubbed down already and was enjoying a bucket of grain. Ears perked up to issue a hello. Checker rubbed the animal on the side of the head and nose.

"You probably don't know what to do with that kind of food, do you, boy. Eating prairie grass is all you've known. An' that's been catch as catch can," Checker said.

Orville Hedrickson, shifting his pipe to the other side of his mouth, came from the back, where he had finished feeding the rest of the stabled horses. His was a modest operation, but one with potential. He carried a lantern high in his skinny arm.

Politely, he asked, "John Checker, vould you like to see our green-broke horses? Fine beasts, they are. As fine as the animal you ride."

"Orville, I've been looking forward to it."

Along came Johnny, swinging his head and grinning,

eager to be around his newly met uncle. His presence served to end the discussion for the moment.

"Come here, hoss, come here," said young Johnny, stepping inside the stall to pet Checker's horse.

"Why, you're going to make me jealous, Johnny. That ol' horse is supposed to only like me," Checker teased.

"We've got one just like this un," the boy said, concentrating on the horse. " 'Cept'n it's brown. An' a mare. Probably shorter too."

The ranger chuckled and turned with Orville to go outside.

"Where are you goin', Uncle John?" Johnny asked.

"Your pa's going to show me some of your horses outside. Want to come with us?"

Johnny's wide smile was the answer.

Checker could tell Orville Hedrickson was a good horseman just by listening to him. The Swede's horses would be gentle, unexcitable, and hard working. The kind every cowboy wanted. His main corral was filled with twenty stock horses, barely taking to the saddle, but all would be excellent mounts, according to the proud Swede.

"They look like a handful to strap leather on right now," Checker observed, leaning his crossed arms on the corral railing.

Orville Hedrickson agreed, surveying his animals with pride, "Yah, if a hoss doesn't buck ya off the first time it's put to the saddle, it won't make much of a hoss. For sure."

Checker nodded then rolled and lit a cigarette. The thin smoke slid into the cool evening air.

"Yah, but breaking the he colt, now that is another colored horse, it is," Orville proclaimed, his eyes moving from the horses to the ranger's face.

"Are you really a Texas Ranger?" Johnny blurted out, no longer able to contain his zeal.

"Well, yes . . . I was," Checker said, "but I left the rangers to help bring a herd of cattle to Dodge City—and to see you."

"Did you kill a lot of bandits?"

Checker didn't know how to answer that question, so he didn't. He pointed out a long-legged dun nipping at a bay in the corral and wondered aloud if it was the leader of the group.

"Supper, boys! Come to the table! Now!" Amelia called to them from the porch, interrupting Orville's response. Checker quickly returned to the barn and grabbed his saddlebags before heading to the house. Tagging along, Johnny eagerly took the saddlebags and carried them for him.

Amelia's table was packed with hot sausages, boiled potatoes, dried apples, rye bread, fresh milk, and honey. White ironstone plates and cups were in place, lined by heavy iron knives and forks. It looked like a feast to Checker. A homecoming feast.

Rebecca stood beside her mother, holding onto a fold in Amelia's dress. The little girl waited expectantly for the tall man she had been told about. As Checker entered the room, Rebecca waddled toward him, her arms outstretched.

"Well, well," Amelia said, pleased at her staging, "I think Rebecca's found her uncle."

Surprised and delighted, Checker laughed and lifted the golden-haired girl. As he held her awkwardly in his arms, Rebecca stared closely at Checker's tanned face; her dainty fingers touched the small arrowhead scar.

"Are you my uncle?" she said, her round eyes so close to his own that he had to move his head backward slightly to see her clearly.

"I sure am, Rebecca," he grinned and kissed her forehead.

Amelia showed Checker where Rebecca was to sit and he eased the little girl into the chair. She was reluctant to leave him. When everyone was seated, Amelia asked her husband to say grace and the passing of food began immediately afterward. Unlike the cow camp Checker had been living in for the last few months, there was hearty conversation throughout the meal. Johnny excitedly described a frog he'd found in the creek; Amelia recounted stories of her and Checker's childhood. The former ranger listened to a world he barely remembered, his sister's view quite different from what he recalled.

Her story of hearing about Texas Ranger John Checker from a passing cowboy was enthusiastically recounted. With her urging, he shared glimpses of his life as a lawman but didn't bring up his earlier days as an outlaw. She didn't ask about the first years after they parted, except to comment on how sad she had been watching him ride away.

Before long, Orville wanted to talk about training stallions, but Amelia's serving of molasses cookies broke the conversation. Even the Swede lost interest in talking, calling the treat *pepparkakor*. The ranger excused himself from the table and went to his saddlebags laying on the floor. He presented his gifts without fanfare. Orville and Amelia seemed pleased, but the reactions of Rebecca and Johnny were pure delight.

Somewhat belatedly, Checker said sheepishly, "I hope that's all right with you, Amelia . . . and Orville. Seemed to me a boy ought to have a knife."

Orville nodded and Amelia said, "Of course." Then she said, "What do you say to your uncle?"

"Gosh, thanks, Uncle John! This is swell. Wait till I show it to Franklin. He didn't believe me when I told him my uncle was a ranger. Boy, will he be jealous!" Rebecca slipped from her chair, holding her new doll, and came over to Checker. He lifted her onto his lap and she kissed the scar on his cheek.

After thanking him for all of the gifts, Amelia asked Checker about the trail drive. He recounted their move-

ment across Texas and the Nations and about his friendship with Dan Mitchell, the foreman. He told them about
the young farm boy, Tyrel Bannon, he had grown to respect. And about Sonny Jones, whose real name he knew
was Cole Dillon and formerly an outlaw on the border. It
was clear he respected the man and honored his change
of life.

That brought the discussion to Dodge City and eventually to their half brother, Star McCallister. Amelia described him more thoroughly than in her letter, but essen-
tially the same.

"It wasn't his fault . . . that his, our, father was—"

"I know."

"No, really, he's a nice man. Quiet. Reserved. Quite the
fine dresser. He's worked hard to be a successful businessman. I hear his place, the Nueces, is a favorite of Texans."

"Would you like to see our creek, Uncle John?" Johnny
asked, no longer able to contain himself.

"Sure, Johnny, I'd like that."

"You mind your manners, young man. We were talking.
You can have plenty of time with your uncle. If he wants
to," Amelia said, hiding a smile.

"How long vill you be staying, John Checker?" Orville
asked. He was using a table knife to open his new can of
tobacco. Amelia gave him a look of annoyance at his
manners.

"The herd's headed for Dodge tomorrow. Mitchell said
I didn't need to come for that. But I want to catch up with
the men . . . in town. Probably the day after."

"Can't that wait for a few more days?" she asked.
"They've had you for a long time. You just got here."

Checker pulled his tobacco pouch and papers from his
shirt pocket and began to roll a smoke. His eyes were
bright, but his face was not readable. A match flame came
alive. He inhaled and changed the subject.

"Any problems with rustlers around here?" he asked without preamble.

Orville puffed on his pipe and answered first, "Nah. I think they are all gone."

"We've heard of a few herds that ran into Indian trouble. But no rustlers," Amelia added.

"That's good to hear," Checker said, then added, "we ran into Kiowas twice. Not too bad. Stole some horses, but we got them back. Lucky, I guess."

CHAPTER 7

THE MOON WASN'T doing much work tonight; the curved sliver was overmatched by sticky gray clouds. Young Tyrel Bannon had actually grown to like riding nighthawk, at least more than most trail hands did.

Something about the quiet appealed to the farm boy. Gave him quiet to really chew on the future, he had decided. At the same time, there was a huge feeling of responsibility, knowing that any wrong move could send the entire herd thundering into the darkness. Tug, the feisty cook, called it "fatherin' the herd."

This was the graveyard watch, midnight to two A.M. A hard one, but better than the "cocktail watch" just before daylight. There, a man had to keep on riding through the day without a break. The two point riders, Jake Woodman and John Checker, were the only hands that never had that shift while on the trail. Dan Mitchell wanted them sharp. At least Bannon had graduated, most of the time, from the "bobtail guard" shift, sundown to eight P.M.

At the campfire tonight, Seals had spoken to Bannon for the first time since the beating. Nervously, he asked why Checker had left camp. Of course, the farm boy had no idea of why or when he might return. Bannon was glad the man seemed ready to forget their fight. But he was surprised at Seals's continued questions about Checker's whereabouts to the others around the fire. Bannon hadn't realized Seals was so concerned about any of the Triple C riders. It was nice though. Maybe everybody was feeling a little sad the drive was coming to an end.

Even more surprising, the surly cowboy had brought out

some bottles of whiskey to celebrate. He said that he'd bought them from a farmer today. Mitchell was already asleep but everyone thought a drink was earned at this point in the drive, and that the trail boss wouldn't mind.

Sonny didn't agree and left the fire. Bannon didn't want to appear like he was rejecting the man's offer of friendship, so he took a small swallow and it burned all the way down his throat.

Bannon had never been a part of anything like this drive before, in his whole life. Down deep, he never wanted the drive to end. But tomorrow it would—with the final push into Dodge City. Well-watered and their bellies filled with grass, the herd would make an impression on the cattle town, he was certain of that.

He had become a man on this ride, respected by his fellow trail hands. He didn't want to be a farmer like his father had been. He wanted to be a cattleman like Dan Mitchell and Mister Carlson. But that dream would have to wait, he realized sadly. His mother would need his help, unless he could make enough pushing cows to offset his not always being around.

No one had said it outright, but he thought Dan Mitchell was impressed with his hard work, his eagerness to learn, to do things right. Bannon thought they would offer him a regular riding job at the Triple C when they got back. Would he be able to take it? He had been chewing on the decision for days now.

Chunks of guilt were mixing in with homesickness and making things real difficult in his mind. Of course, it was definitely putting the cart before the horse. No one had asked him yet, he advised silently.

Riding slowly, circling the herd, he shyly sang a verse of "Buffalo Gal." The song was little more than a pushed whisper. Singing made him self-conscious, as if anyone was listening. He wished he knew more than one verse. Hearing his voice was nice, not that it was a thing of beauty. Rather thin, actually. Still, singing felt good.

Mitchell and Jackson had taught him that it was important to keep the herd comfortable and feeling safe with him there. Singing was part of it. Kept a cowboy awake too. The song was one of his mother's favorites. She liked it because his father had, or so she said.

Jackson was on the west side of the herd, barely visible in the darkness, headed slowly Bannon's way. Jackson's baritone voice was so fine and smooth the young rider often stopped his own singing to listen. Quite different than his own reedy warbling. Jackson's steady, quiet way was a style Bannon had grown to like. Both rode in opposite directions, loosely around the herd. Keeping forty to fifty feet from any animal. Four other riders—Freddie Tucker, Clanahan, Tex and Sonny Jones—were watching the herd. Without saying anything, the black cowboy rode up and stopped. Jackson's hands rested on the pommel as he leaned forward in the saddle. He wanted to talk. Bannon stopped his horse in response. Furrows in Jackson's brow were easy enough to read; he was worried.

"Not right tonight, Ty," Jackson said matter-of-factly, like he was describing a hurt animal. "Something's around. Feel it. Something bad."

"Jackson, everything seems . . . herd's quiet. Real quiet. Maybe you're just tired," the young man replied in his most comforting voice.

Jackson's look was one of silent understanding of Bannon's attempt to make him feel better, without accepting the young man's words as knowledgeable.

"Don't use any matches. Watch the dark, not the beeves, Ty," he said. "I remember the time a nighthawk, young fella like you, he lit a match and that was all she wrote. Bang, the whole herd's up an' running. Took us two days to round them up again. Must have been three hundred dead. Ran over each other they were so wound up. Crazy things."

"Why would this herd run? They're fat an' happy here, Jackson."

The black man gritted his teeth in frustration, before answering, "I'll say it another way, Tyrel. A match lights up a man from a long way. Makes him an easy target for someone good with a rifle."

With that, the black man clucked his horse and walked away.

"Watch good, Ty Bannon. Into the dark. Into the dark," Jackson said, his back turned. The way he said the words, it could have been a song or something out of one of his books.

Soon the blond-haired young rider heard him singing again. It was comforting. Bannon rode past a group of muleys. Off to itself, but not moving, was a thin-flanked brown cow with head down and jaw swollen. Rattlesnake bite. The young rider felt sorry for the animal; there wasn't anything to be done. The animal would either live through the poison or die.

Yesterday, he'd overheard Dan Mitchell say a few steers looked "sage," sick from eating sage. That comment ran through his mind, and his curiosity made him study each steer he passed. But he couldn't tell which ones they were. It gave him something to do to pass the time, though. Then he remembered Jackson's warning and looked away from the resting animals toward the darkened surroundings.

Scattered around the edges of the grass were wild tulip and larkspur. Invisible now, but he knew they were there. They always reminded him of his mother; she would gush over their colors like they were jewels. Down one long shadowed draw were white blossoms of wild pea with splashes of red current. He couldn't see them now, either. And far away was a long strip of forest sitting on that meandering ridge. Like huge black fingers holding the grassland in place. Really something to see, he thought. In daylight, of course. Not now.

Off to the south was a winding staircase of stone, like something out of a Southern mansion he had once found in a neighbor's picture book, only a lot bigger. It was more or less connected to the fat creek. He wanted to come back and climb it some day.

The ghostlike whiteness of the rock reminded him of the eerie sight they had passed when leaving the Cimarron River. A long line of buffalo skulls, white and staring at the sky, pointed the way to Dodge. A scattering of other bones left him wondering why all those animals had to be killed. He wondered what seeing a big herd of buffalo must've been like. Then his mind drifted again.

"Everything looks fine to me," he muttered to himself. "Jackson's just jumpy. Not like him. Maybe he's sad it's about over too."

Wild onions had been added to the evening supper, making a tasty meal of roasted quail, biscuits, and beans. Quail were plentiful in the long hedgerows. Bannon had bagged ten this morning with Tug's shotgun. For a special treat, Sonny Jones had bought three apple pies from a nearby farm. Those pies had disappeared like they were inhaled.

Bannon was burping those onions in rhythm to his singing, sort of. Mainly burping. Or was it the swallow of the fiery brown liquid? It smelled bad. When he got off nighthawking, his teeth would be given a serious brushing with a bark-peeled stick he carried for such a chore, maybe putting some baking soda on it, if Tug would give him some from the chuck wagon.

His turn would be over in a couple of hours. Pete Foster was to follow him. Bannon had learned to wake him easylike; the oldtimer tended to wake up with a pistol in his hand, ready for a fight. Right from the start, Dan Mitchell had taught the young rider to wake a man by talking to him, not by touching him. In a trail drive like this had been, he was likely to come up with a gun in his hand. The foreman had wryly said that it didn't matter much if the man shot him, it was just what the shot would do to the herd.

The night was getting colder; high prairie wind was adding to the coolness. He rolled his shoulders and let a shiver rip along his back. Movement! Out of the corner of his eye, he saw something move over by the dry creek bed some twenty yards from him. A flicker of gray against gray. The rock-lined crack had split off from the big stream long ago and paid for its independence with no permanent water following. A coyote, maybe. Slowly he swung his horse around to look.

Nothing. Must have been his imagination. Boy, that was easy to have happen. A man, especially a young one, could conjure up all kinds of things waiting for him in the darkness. No, that wasn't it. No, not really. He was sure something had moved along the ridge. Indians? Could there be Indians moving in on them? As he studied the creek bed, he drew the Walker Colt; its rhythmic click a reassuring message.

Moonlight flickered off metal near a bush resting on what had been the upper bank. A rifle barrel! What the heck is going on? Too early for anyone to relieve the guards. Surely nobody would be wandering over there with a gun. In the dark, he heard Captain growl.

Suddenly gunshots broke into the quiet from where Sonny Jones was guarding at the northwest edge of the herd. What was he doing? The herd would explode! Bannon turned in the saddle to peer into the darkness. Another shot came from over near the remuda, and the farm boy heard horses running and whinnying.

"Ambush!" The yell was Sonny's, punctuated by a roar of gunfire—from everywhere! Any other words, by any-

one, were drowned by the battery of orange flames ripping
into the night. A dozen firing points flashed from that dry
creek bed where it cut near the camp. More gunfire sought
the night guards wherever they stood with the herd.

Bullets whined their deadly songs past Bannon's head
and shoulders. One bit the pommel of his saddle. Another
clipped the shirt at his elbow. His turning had been
enough to save his life. Deadly rifle fire tore the night into
shreds and pounded into sleeping men. His friends!

Bannon spun his horse and hammered it toward the
creek, firing his heavy Colt at the shadows behind the
never-ending orange flames. Behind the young rider,
Freddie Tucker flew from his saddle and lay unmoving on
the trembling ground; Tex's horse reared, screamed, and
both animal and rider crumpled. Cattle were jumping,
bawling, and crashing into each other. They began to run
madly away from the noise. Stampede!

From inside the camp came two yellow bursts followed
by a loud *boom-boom*. Tug! And his shotgun! The shouts of
his friends were swallowed by the wall of gunfire. Sonny's
loud curse made it over the thunder. The only one. Thick-
ening smoke made it impossible to tell where the former
outlaw was. Down near the front of the herd, Bannon
thought.

A few camp shots were answering the solid line of fire from
the arroyo, but not many. Going in the opposite direction
of the young rider, Jackson raced to reach Sonny and the
head of the stampeding herd. Everything was a blur of
sounds, shadows, and flashes in the night-enshrouded
madness encircling them. Low across the neck of his horse,
the black cowboy's eyes squinted to discern innocent
shadow from deadly shadow.

Beside him was Harry Clanahan. Grim-eyed and taut-
faced, the Irishman rode hunkered in the saddle, swearing
at the top of his lungs.

"Bleeming bastards! God-damn bleeming bastards!" the dark-haired Clanahan spat as he hammered his heels in the bay to keep up with Jackson's smooth-running mount.

Jackson glanced back in response to the Irishman's colorful spouting. There was nothing like the brogue of an Irishman, especially in battle. Clanahan was a good man to have at your backside, he thought.

Tex and Freddie Tucker had gone down in the first volley of shots; Jackson had seen that. But he had no idea about Bannon or Sonny—or the camp itself. A flicker of what might be happening to Dan Mitchell, to his friends, was all he would allow himself. To dwell on this possible agony would serve only to distract him from trying to save the herd.

His plan was for Clanahan—hopefully, Sonny—and himself to get in front of the desperate animals, slow them into a leadable group, and guide them quickly to some unexpected place—before the full force of the rustlers caught up.

Maybe Bannon would eventually make it, too. Together, they might make the price too high for the rustlers and they would leave. His only other choice was to return to camp and fight there. Without belaboring the thought, Jackson knew it was already too late for that.

Crazed steers skittered mindlessly yards ahead of him, but most of the herd was now at his heels. His thick-shouldered horse was eating up the dark plains to regain the lead. Outstretched, the animal was running smoothly, loving the fury of battle. Its elegant neck was low and extended, its teeth clinched in commitment, its breath appearing in pale clouds.

Clanahan's horse was as game as its rider, just not as strong. Jackson could hear its labored wheezing coming in rhythm to their running. They couldn't worry about stepping into a prairie-dog hole or sliding on a slick patch of grass and get in front of the splintered herd.

It was one or the other. If either horse hit something like that, the rider and mount would both likely die. Or they would be so badly injured that the rustlers would handle them with ease, and they would die that way too. That choice had been made: get into the lead. The loyal black man felt he owed it to Dan Mitchell and Charlie Carlson. They had always trusted him. Clanahan had sand and wouldn't have wished for it to be any other way; he rode for the brand.

An orange blossom suddenly appeared off to their left, then another and another. Bullets hummed past Jackson, in the lead. More ambushers! One bullet drilled a hole through his flapping long coat; another bit the pommel of his saddle. In response, he snapped a shot just to the right of the last gunburst. He fired again and again at the same imagined point as he galloped on. Thick gunsmoke filled his nostrils.

A shuddered cry cut through the night, "By the Mither of Saints, I . . ."

The reason registered in his brain as the words reached his ears. Clanahan had been hit! He reined in the sweating horse, but not too hard. The animal was running all-out but still responded. Jackson swung him around and charged back toward the trees where the firing had come from.

His Colt sought the shadows that didn't mesh with the trees. Wham! Wham! Wham! His first three shots were quick as one man stepped from behind a tree to fire his rifle. The man shuddered with the impact of Jackson's shots, sat down, and looked at the red seeping onto his shirt.

With the immediate danger removed, the black cowboy rode to Clanahan, laying still, his leg under the downed horse. The powerful rear legs of Jackson's mustang slammed into the prairie dirt as he brought it to a halt beside the Irishman. Jackson pushed the pistol into his holster and jumped down, suspecting the worst. He held the reins of his own horse as a precaution; steers were thundering past on both sides and the mustang might find it hard to resist.

The battle was fierce in the mustang's nostrils and the big horse yanked on the reins, prancing and snorting, resenting the curtailing of the attack. He sympathized with the animal, appreciating its courage, calming it with his steadying words.

Jackson's voice was low. "Easy, boy. Easy now. We've got to be smart, Easy now." Gradually the mustang stood still. He patted its neck with appreciation.

Dazed, the Irishman blinked and said, "Jackson, ye must be a blitherin' angel. Have I gone to heaven . . . to see me blessed mither?"

"Not yet, you crazy mick," Jackson said. "Can you move?"

"Go on, Jackson. Go on. Ye might still turn 'em. By the saints, man, go!" Clanahan said, regaining his senses and beginning to push on the dead horse with his free leg.

"Here, let me help. You're going with me. Ol' Joe can carry us both."

Jackson shoved against the dead horse, gradually giving Clanahan enough room to pull his injured leg from underneath. Shock was eating into his grit. Jackson didn't try to examine the wound; there was only time to get his friend in the saddle. Treating it would have to wait. Jackson was proud of his big horse, blowing and sweating and wanting to run. It stood quietly in place, as if understanding the need to get the wounded man on his back fast.

Jackson shoved Clanahan's boot into the left stirrup and hefted him upward. Jackson held the quivering cowboy as the Irishman stepped into the stirrup, grabbed the saddle horn, and tried to lift his sagging body onto the horse's back. His left leg wobbled as he swung the other leg up.

Jackson's shoulder took on Clanahan's full weight to keep him from falling; he shoved the Irishman's limp leg over and pushed him squarely into the saddle.

The black man's eye glasses caught on the Irishman's shoulder and fell. Frantically, he swept the ground with his hand, found the spectacles, and held them in his fist. Swinging up behind Clanahan, Jackson whistled the animal into action. It responded as if the double weight was nothing. Ground-eating strides dissolved them into the night. Up a rock-strewn hill Jackson's horse glided as if it were on level ground.

Jackson and Clanahan were separated from Bannon now by a quarter mile, hundreds of steers, and a long-running hill. The young rider was aware only of the savage shooting in front of him. His chest pounded like a hawk inside him, fiercely flapping its wings. His eyes were bright with battle. Sweat peppered his face; his blond hair was wet, strands stuck to his damp cheeks.

But his vision was enhanced. His actions were quicker, controlled by an unknown force. His instincts were linked to things felt, not seen. Everything and everyone seemed to be moving in slow motion. Fear wasn't allowed within. He didn't believe he would be killed.

Closing to the edge of the creek, Bannon fired again at the shadow behind a flickering orange flame. A yowl of pain followed. Flame came his way. He heard the bullet near his shoulder. Again, he cocked the gun as his horse leaped down into the creek bed.

The charging animal slammed against one shadow. Bannon fired at the man and another, as horse and rider bounded through the small arroyo and raced up the other side. And away. Wheeling his horse for a return charge, he fired back at the row of ambushers now split between shooting at the camp and stopping him. The hammer struck a faulty cartridge. He recocked it as his horse raced back toward the war. Bullets were angry bees of lead around him.

Holding the pistol out like it was a part of his arm, he tried to spot unseen targets. Downward, his horse exploded underneath him. The sickening thud of a rifle bullet in the animal's chest was the only warning an instant before it collapsed.

His feet flew backward and his body forward. The horse caught itself and straightened up, throwing its powerful neck backward in a fierce desire to go on. Off-balance and extended far forward to stay in the saddle, Bannon's face crunched against the sledgehammer neck and he went out.

The last thing he remembered was being dragged, his boot caught in a stirrup, as his severely wounded horse turned and fled instinctively from the creek bed. West and away from the shooting. Bannon's head thudded against a rock outcropping until he passed out. About the same time, his horse stopped running, stumbled, and fell to the ground. Several times the horse tried to rise before it succumbed to the rifle wound.

The night attack went on, but Bannon lay unseeing and unknowing. Lightning flashed in the far distance, dancing closer by the minute. Thick drops began to pelt the stampeded prairie and the camp. Soon rain was hammering the Kansas earth. Lightning crashed again on the neck of a long slope nearly a mile away, turning the uppermost ridge golden for a heartbeat and highlighting two men on a horse. The loud crack of its violence trailed by another heartbeat. Then everything returned to darkness. All night sounds were destroyed by the storm's roaring song.

Farther to the north, hidden within a grove of trees, a lone rider cursed his played-out horse and his empty guns. Beyond Sonny Jones by another half mile, the bandits worked to bring thousands of cattle back into a unit before moving them on.

* * *

The rain let up only at sunrise. Sometime in the early morning, Tyrel Bannon awoke with the night's horror driving his first reactions. He grabbed for his pistol as if the time between falling and now had been an eye blink. But the holster was empty. His Colt lay next to a large clump of sage; the handle cradled in soft sand.

Standing quickly to get it brought a dizziness that pushed him to the earth almost as fast as he had stood. He vomited into the wet dirt. Crouching on his hands and knees, he tried to keep the world from spinning away. He passed out again.

A curious coyote brought him around by sniffing at his bloodied ear. The animal ran as soon as its point of interest moved. Groggy, Bannon fought for consciousness again. It was midmorning, judging from where the sun was looking at him. His clothes were wet; his shirt was torn from being dragged. A dark blood spot stood out in the middle of a large, flat rock near him. It was one of many stones along a long, low slope. The blood was his.

More slowly this time, he stood. His fingers felt the place on his forehead where he'd hit the rock. Dried blood crumbled under the touch. Pain throbbed in his temples like those Cheyenne war drums Clanahan was jawing about a few nights back. He shook his head to clear away the pounding. It didn't help. But this time he was able to get his Colt and add new loads without passing out.

Northwest a hundred yards was the campsite. Mechanically, he turned to look there. Nothing moving, except for eight grazing steers and three loose horses. How could this be?! Everybody should be moving about, talking, laughing, cursing, drinking coffee. Something should be happening. Tug should be working on breakfast. Randy should be roping horses. Dan Mitchell should be talking with Checker and Jackson. Woodman should be massaging his feet.

With a sigh, he turned back to his dead horse and gave

it a pat on the head. But the young cowboy couldn't keep ignoring the real thing that was wrong. He took tentative steps to see if the ground was cooperating, then began an uneven walk toward the eerily quiet campsite. The rain had washed the ground clean of footprints and horse's hooves, giving the earth a fresh start and adding to Bannon's sense of loss.

It took a half hour to cover the short distance, wobbling forward and sitting to wait until the lightheadedness left, getting up again, wobbling forward and sitting again. He repeated the process all the way to the southern tip of the dry creek bed. He stumbled three times, vomiting once.

His mind accepted the bodies of Elias Harrelson and Israel Rankin first. They had died in their bedrolls. Beside them was an empty whiskey bottle. He was surprised to see it, since the foreman had been quite clear about no drinking in camp. Except on very special occasions that he determined. Then he recalled Seals had foolishly passed it.

Pausing only to make certain of what his eyes already told him, he walked on. A handful of arrows, two tomahawks, and a feather-laden lance were laying about this death camp. Two arrows were stuck in the ground close together; the other four were scattered about.

"Indians! Red savages did this!" he exclaimed. He swallowed the discovery and swung his arms without purpose, trying to wail away the ache.

He stopped and called out a terrified string of names into the open miles of green grass and gray sky. "Boss! Dan Mitchell! Jackson! Randy! Tex! Sonny! Boss! Dan Mitchell! Tug! Jake! Sonny! Randy! Pete! Dan!"

Not even Mitchell's three-legged dog answered. Perhaps they were sleeping after the awful night. Perhaps it was just a bad dream. No. There was no denying any more what he saw. The herd was gone. That brought a hard edge to what he already knew was true but did not want to admit. No one would be sleeping if the herd was missing. No, they were dead. The raiders had taken the horses too.

The chuck wagon was a charred mess with four wheels sticking up, like some big black animal had melted and left its black bones. The rain didn't come soon enough to save much. Only the calf wagon had been spared the fire's wrath.

Near the sagging remuda corral rope was Jacob Webster. The already injured man had gotten there somehow before being cut down. He had no gun. Bannon screamed into the uncaring sky, as long and as loud as he could. Until it made him dizzy again. The clouding of his mind took him to a blackness, somewhere where he was lost. When he woke up, the sun was signaling noon to the silent bodies. He swallowed and forced himself to investigate further.

Stuart Willis hadn't made it out of his bedroll either. Neither had Wonson. A half-empty whiskey bottle was cradled in a shallow wallow beside his body. Jake Woodman looked like he had tried to put on his boots and pants before shooting back. Bannon cursed Seals for the whiskey.

"Pete Foster, you ol' wolf," he spoke into the afternoon air as he moved to the old drover's body. "You went at 'em right from your bedroll. Probably too stiff to move. Bet they had a helluva time puttin' you down."

Foster had made a fight of it; his Winchester lay beside his lifeless elbow. Empty. His pistol, also empty, was held tightly in death. A dozen shell casings were strewn about his bedroll battle station. The grizzled old-timer had proved himself a fighting man right down to the last.

He must've taken a bunch of the red devils with him, the young rider observed with an odd feeling of pride. But there weren't any dead Indians anywhere that Bannon could see. He remembered Checker telling him they carried their dead away.

His friends. Dead. Killed, trying to fight back from an unmerciful sneak attack by bloodthirsty Indians. He walked among them, stunned. Like walking inside an awful oil painting. This couldn't be! It was the first time Tyrel Bannon remembered ever crying. He hadn't when his father died although the sorrow was locked in his throat for a long time.

"Who could do this? Why didn't they kill me?" he suddenly asked himself aloud, his lower lip trembling and his voice quivering. Guilt drove deep into his soul. The killers must have forgotten about him, since he ended up so far away from camp.

He turned from the sight. He just couldn't take anymore. It had to be an ugly dream. It had to be. His friends lay so still with their own blood masking white faces, unseeing eyes staring at the fading sun. It was worse than any nightmare. He wanted to see his mother, to have her tell him it was only a bad dream. A deep breath didn't help. He gagged, pulling hard to get in the air that would give him enough strength to keep from retching.

That made him recall his own shooting, and he walked in a zigzag line to the edge of the creek bed. His head continued to ache without relenting. No bodies. But dark blotches on the rocks showed he hadn't missed. A few moccasin prints also had evaded the rain's demands.

Movement! Vultures! His brain raced with an anger erasing the pain in his head. He drew his old Colt. The walnut grips felt good in his hand. Two quick shots dropped two birds; his third missed. The rest of the ugly creatures of death escaped to the sky. To wait. He dropped the gun a foot from the shallow crevice and returned to his dead friends.

Never had he seen death like this. In fact, the only death the young man had witnessed was his father's. That awful picture came now to haunt him, making a silent hell of the silent camp. All of it beyond understanding. How could anyone do something like this? When would he wake up and hear his friends talking and laughing again?

Three dead horses were laying in the corral; their bellies swelling. A fourth dead animal was Dan Mitchell's; its bloated frame rested in the middle of camp. Saddled and bridled, it was the trail boss's best night horse, the one he kept ready each night, next to where he slept.

Beside the animal was Dan Mitchell himself, facedown on the wet ground. Unmoving like the others. The night's downpour had not been successful in removing every trace of red in the soil around him. He had slept fully clothed, including his boots and pistol belt, and was soaking wet. Mitchell's Winchester was inches away; the lever was swung open as if ejecting a spent shell. Lying down against the silent trail boss was Captain, unhurt but whimpering softly.

Bannon knelt beside Mitchell and held his red-soaked face in his arms. Tears slid down his tanned cheeks again. Captain nuzzled his back, easing the young man's anguish. Slowly he lifted Mitchell's head and turned his body on its side. A soft groan was the most wonderful sound he thought he'd ever heard! Then another.

Dan Mitchell was breathing! Dan Mitchell was still alive!

Grabbing a canteen from the saddle of Mitchell's dead horse, the farm boy poured its contents onto his kerchief and began clearing away the caked blood and dried mud half-covering the cowman's face. The blood came from a long angry crease dug alongside his right ear. A half-inch closer and he was very dead. He had bullet wounds in his right shoulder and in the lower right arm. Little of his shirt wasn't covered with blood or mud.

After cleaning Mitchell's scalp, Bannon worked on his arm, carefully pulling the shirt fragments from the encrusted hole, trickling blood. The bullet had passed cleanly through, and it didn't look like it had struck any bone. At least not solidly. Then he tore away the shirt and cleaned the shoulder wound as best he could. Small pieces of the cloth were driven deep into the angry hole. The slug was in there too. Mitchell was going to need real doctoring and soon. At least it wasn't festering. Yet.

Seeing nothing closeby that would work better, the young rider tore off his own dried shirtsleeve to make bandage strips. He wrapped three discarded bedroll blankets around the unconscious trail boss.

Mitchell shouldn't be in those wet pants, Bannon knew, but he thought it best to get a fire going first for warmth. The dying sun was taking the day's heat with it. Disturbing the man right now to change his shirt and pants just didn't make sense to him either. A small sack of dry kindling and matches was found in Mitchell's saddlebags. Bannon expected as much.

The young rider remembered Mitchell, Jackson, Woodman, and Checker always carrying such things. At Tug's "possum belly" under the charred chuck wagon, he happily discovered the fire hadn't come close and the cook's emergency fuel supply was intact—and mostly dry. Grabbing a handful of dried buffalo chips, he turned and was startled to see Tug himself.

Apparently, the little man had been sitting on the other side of the chuck wagon all along. He was disoriented but not hurt; dried biscuit dough lined his forearms and spotted his face. His clothes were etched with soot from the fire. Bannon guessed he had been working on breakfast when the attack came. There was a red swelling on Tug's forehead. Bannon decided the feisty cook had knocked himself out trying to find cover when the attack came. He would ask Tug about it later.

"Tug! Tug, are you all right?" the young rider exclaimed.

"Son, I . . . what happened . . . to us?"

"Indians."

"I'm afraid breakfast . . . is gonna . . . be late, son. When do . . . we hit . . . the trail?" Tug looked around the camp. "Where's Mitchell? He'll be mad as hell at me."

"The boss is hurt . . . bad. But he's alive. Come on, I was fixin' a fire for him," Bannon said loudly, expecting Tug's lack of hearing to be worse. It was. The young rider repeated himself three times, pointing to Mitchell and the fire for emphasis.

Finally, Tug rubbed his nose with his finger and said, "Dammit, boy, I heared ya the first time. No need to make like a canyon. I ain't deaf, ya know." Bannon couldn't resist a small grin.

Soon the farm boy had a small fire crackling ten feet from Mitchell. Pieces of downed wood lay atop, first to dry and then to give themselves to the flames. Tug sat beside the warmth, staring into it. The young rider couldn't be sure, but thought Mitchell was resting more easily now, sleeping and not unconscious. That was probably just wishful thinking, he told himself.

Yet the veteran cowman was a tough man. If anyone could make it through this, he could. The look and sound of the tiny fire was comforting as Bannon realized for the first time he was very hungry. He thought for a moment about asking Tug, but knew the cook wasn't ready to handle any task yet. Turning his attention to a search through the burned-out wagon, he found that some of the food hadn't been destroyed.

Most of a sackful of potatoes was untouched. The corners of two salt pork slabs appeared usable. None of the flour was even close to being white, but he found three tins of hard biscuits. Half a sack of dried beans were tiny cinders, but the rest looked edible. The coffee sack had survived; it was outside the wagon. And six cans of peaches. The rest was black and unrecognizable as food.

Coffee was soon smelling good from a small blackened pot. Slices of salt pork went into the skillet. Bannon munched on a hard biscuit and ate a peach from an opened can while he cooked. He cut two potatoes into chunks and added them to the sizzling meat. A slice of the pork, after it had been frying awhile, was tossed to an eager Captain. The young rider blew on the meat first so it wouldn't be too hot.

Bannon tried to lose himself in the cooking but just being here was unsettling and wrong. *Should I ride to town tonight for a doctor? What if the Indians came back while I'm gone . . . Dan Mitchell and Tug would be helpless. Should I try to take them to town . . . in the calf wagon? Could Mitchell make it? Could I get two of those horses rigged up to pull it? Ma always told me to take time to think. Seemed like she was always reminding me of that. Thinking, that was the only thing separating people from animals, she liked to say.*

Mitchell stirred. At first, Bannon thought it was the early wings of night playing a cruel trick, then it came again. He stepped away from the fire and kneeled beside the wounded man.

"T-T-Ty? That you, Ty?" came a low, guttural voice as Dan Mitchell blinked his eyes and tried to rise up on his elbows. Instantly, jolting pain in his right arm and shoulder drove him to the ground, gasping for air.

"It's me . . . boss," the young man said quietly. "You've been shot. Purty bad."

"The herd, did they . . . ?"

"Yeah. Herd's gone. Tug's here. Looks like he got knocked out. They got everyone else in camp. Except, maybe, Seals, Reilman. Haven't found them anyway. Don't know about the other nighthawks. Haven't seen anybody."

Bannon held Mitchell's head up enough to make it easier for him to drink some of the tepid canteen water. His folded kerchief was dampened and placed on Mitchell's forehead as they talked. In short phrases, the young rider recapped the ambush as best he knew it. But his knowledge of the herd itself stopped at the stampede.

"Can you eat somethin'? It'd be good for you."

"N-N-No. Not now. Too tired, Ty. Need to sleep. Then I'll—"

"Dan, I've got to get you to town. You need a doc. Bullet's still in your shoulder. Can—"

"I can ride. Give me a little more time. Morning. I understand," he spoke without emotion, then paused. "Son . . . we can't leave these men like this. I . . ."

"I know," Bannon said, giving him more sips of water. "I'll take care of the burying. Tonight."

"Ty?"

"Yessir?"

"If you can find some moss, pack it on these here bullet holes. Injun medicine. Leave it on till the sawbones sees me."

"I'll do it. Should be some by the creek," the young man said. Then he thought about it and added, "It was Indians that hit us. Signs all over."

CHAPTER 8

BEFORE MITCHELL COULD respond, the wounded foreman drifted back to sleep. Realizing the conversation was over, Bannon went to find moss and returned in minutes with both hands full of the moist covering. He rebandaged Mitchell's shoulder, as the trail boss mumbled incoherently about things the crew needed to do with the herd.

"Ohhhh! What a stupid . . . !" the young cowboy cursed himself for forgetting about the cooking meat and potatoes. When he returned to the fire, smoke was curling from the skillet, and some of the meat and potato chunks looked more like cinders than food. He grabbed for the skillet handle but quickly thought better of it.

"Hmm! Hot! Of course it's hot, stupid," he said to himself and tried again to lift the pan from the fire; this time wrapping the handle in the flap of his right chap. He set the scorched skillet on the ground and stared at it in disgust. But hunger overcame his irritation, so he studied the intended meal and decided some pieces looked like they might be worth eating.

Bannon set a plate of food beside Tug. Then Bannon gobbled down anything that wasn't entirely burnt. Afterward, he wiped his forehead and mouth with his remaining dirty sleeve. His stomach hadn't minded the overcooking so much; it was better than nothing. Although he admitted the peaches and hard biscuits were the best part of the meal. Tug hadn't eaten anything. He still sat beside the fire.

As darkness fell, Bannon felt last night was starting all over again somehow. He removed his old hat, letting cooling air dance across his sweaty blond hair and clear his mind of the ghosts. It was time for burying, something he wasn't looking forward to. But he wouldn't be able to sleep anyway.

First, he forced himself to check each man's body, gathering letters or special things a family might want as keepsakes. Like Webster's prized buckle and Woodman's fancy spurs. The letter Harrelson kept folded in his shirt pocket. He didn't know who had family and who didn't, or where they'd be, or if he'd ever be able to find them—but trying seemed like the right thing to do. These things he put in an unburned sack he found in the chuck wagon, one Tug had used to hold apples. There were a dozen apples left; all cooked to some extent or another. He would save them for the morning.

Any money he found went into the sack, too. He kept track of the amounts. Using the trail boss's own stubby pencil, he wrote each man's accounting on a page of the foreman's pocket pad. Taking other people's things gave him a long pause. But the only other option was to bury these things along with the men, and that didn't make much sense.

After this gathering was done, he began rummaging for a shovel through the burned remains of the chuck wagon. Out of the ashes, he uncovered one; only the top part of the handle had been seared. The crew's extra gear and war bags—all blackened embers—had been on top of the shovel and had kept the flames at bay. He recalled a small metal box that contained the ownership papers for the herd, plus some other papers Mitchell had. It should have survived the fire, but there was no sign of it anywhere.

Laying the foreman's Winchester close by, he began digging where the ground seemed easiest, figuring on one large grave. It was hard work, but his mind and body needed this. Maybe the other nighthawks, or Seals or Reilman—or even John Checker—would show up before he was finished. It was a comfort to think others had survived, but he didn't allow himself to count on it.

Even in the cool night air, he shed his shirt an hour into the task. Two coyotes sneaked up to watch, brought there by the growing smell of death.

"Get outta here, you mangy coyotes!" he yelled, sending them scurrying.

The fresh air across his sweating chest felt good. He broke from the task only once to drink from the stream and put his head in its wetness. He wrapped each body in a blanket, which made it easier to pull them to the grave and kept him from having to stare at the lifeless remains. He tied Pete Foster's kerchief around his face to cut down the penetrating odor.

Gradually, he came to realize that he must take Mitchell and Tug to town in the calf wagon. The wounded man could never stay in a saddle, no matter how much he might want to. And he wasn't certain what to expect from Tug.

Better that the trail boss lay in the wagon bed and be somewhat comfortable. Of course, that was assuming two of the loose horses could be caught—and would put up with pulling the wagon. The spirited animals wouldn't likely care much for it.

Pausing to catch his breath, he noticed Captain was standing five feet away, watching. The dog cocked his head as if trying to understand what the young rider was saying under his breath. Leaning on the shovel, Bannon explained his statement to the animal, who seemed interested. "Captain, we're gonna have to take the boss—and Tug—to town. Agree?"

But maybe tomorrow would bring Checker, Jackson, and the rest riding into camp. Smiling and pushing the herd in front of them. He spat, then looked at the night sky just starting to sprout stars. He knew it wasn't true.

After filling back the dirt, Bannon dragged rocks from the dry bed and placed them over the burial mound. Once, as he was gathering a load of rocks, it sounded like riders were coming. A low rumbling came from across the big ridge. Grabbing the rifle, he lay next to the freshly filled grave. The cock of the hammer cracked the silence. He waited. Nothing happened. Maybe it was a herd of buffalo running, he thought and finally stood.

Bannon checked on Mitchell and Tug before giving in to sleep. Captain woke him before dawn, licking his face. He cooked another round of sliced salt pork, potatoes, and the apples he'd found, serving some to Mitchell and Tug. Both ate a little, although Bannon couldn't tell if Mitchell didn't have much of an appetite yet or if the man couldn't handle the young cowboy's cooking.

Bannon wasn't too fond of it himself. Captain got plenty to eat. The happiest moment came when Tug hollered out, "Damn, this is poor! You can't cook for nothing, Tyrel!"

With that, the cook stood up and went to give Mitchell some water. The gritty foreman had lost more blood than a man should and be alive, but he was holding on. Sounding more and more like his old self, Tug tended to Mitchell while Bannon hid the extra saddles and guns in the rock staircase, covering them with a blanket, rocks, and branches. He kept Woodman's Winchester for himself. It was smart and practical to do, but the keeping bothered him anyway. It just didn't seem right, but he convinced himself that the detail-minded point rider would have wanted it that way.

He threw Mitchell's saddle and his own into the calf wagon, along with both rifles. The unburned saddlebags from the chuck wagon, or laying with the tack, were also stowed. Lastly, he added the sack of things he had collected as well as Tug's shotgun and five live loads he had found.

Before leaving, Tug and Bannon stood over the grave with heads bowed. Mitchell had drifted into unconsciousness. Tug broke down and wept. Captain stood beside the young cowboy. Bannon's hat was gripped tightly in both hands; his body trembled. Jackson had the only Bible he knew of, so he tried to remember something his mother had asked him to memorize as a boy.

"Now I lay down in green pastures . . . where the water's good and cool. I don't fear nothin', God, because you're ridin' with me . . ."

He stopped. There weren't any more words coming, no matter how hard he searched for them. Grief burned his eyes and tears stained his cheeks.

"God, these are my friends. They didn't deserve to die. No how. I will find their killers, God. If you'll ride with me, that is. Like your words say. Leastwise, you be ridin' with Dan Mitchell, 'cause he needs fixin', you hear. Amen."

Tug said quietly, "Goodbye, boys."

As if understanding the need, one of Sonny's mounts, a sturdy brown mustang with a white stocking on the right foreleg, immediately came to the young rider, its head down. Bannon slipped a noose around the horse's neck and led it to the creek for watering.

The two remaining horses, a big sorrel and a bay, trotted along, but they were skittish and shied away from him. He knew his roping skills weren't up to catching them, but one of them would be needed since the old wagon was a two-horse hitch. The big sorrel came toward him as if this was a game, tossing its head lightly and dancing on eager feet.

"Come on, you dang red hoss. I ain't got the time."

The animal looked disappointed at his lack of interest. As Bannon lead the mustang back from the water, the red horse nuzzled his arm and seemed relieved when he finally put a lariat over its neck and tied it to one of the picket trees where the sagging rope corral was stationed. The bay wasn't sure yet. That was fine.

As Tyrel Bannon hesitantly laced the bridling on the two horses, he felt a swell of eagerness, partly to get away from this awful place of death, but mostly because he couldn't wait to get to Dodge City. After finding a doctor for Dan

Mitchell, he would go to the town law. Surely the sheriff would call for a posse, and Bannon wanted to lead the charge.

With Tug's help, Bannon lifted Mitchell and laid him in the back of the wagon. Tug straightened the blankets around the unconscious foreman. Then the stumpy cook climbed onto the seat, followed by the farm boy. Bannon clucked to the horses, and they jerked at their unfamiliar traces. The sorrel reared, but the brown mustang moved out as if it had always pulled a wagon. Soon they were headed jerkily toward Dodge City.

Dawn was flirting with John Checker as he rode slowly through a muddy arroyo. His sister's homestead was two miles back. Last night's rain had turned the lowlands into a syrupy mire. Horse and rider could slip and be hurt quickly if both weren't careful. Still, it was the horse that was doing most of the tending to the conditions. Checker's mind was filled with the wonder of the reunion.

Never in his life could he recall such a thrill. Seeing Amelia's son and daughter was like looking into a memory. Everything within him was sweet and fulfilled. And nothing in him wanted to leave. But he had promised to meet the Triple C men in town. Not only that, he wanted to be there at the drive's successful conclusion. These men had become his friends, especially Dan Mitchell. As soon as they left for Texas, he would return to his sister's place for a few days. Then he would decide what was next. Maybe he would settle around here. The thought titillated his imagination.

Even though his thinking was focused elsewhere, the practiced skill of a man long used to riding into danger kept him in the low seams of the land, however soggy, avoiding any ridge that might skyline his presence. The plains were soon glowing yellow, like apple cider had been poured over the land. His big horse eased along the side of a winding creek, fat from rain, lined by tall blue stem grass and mothered by a thick grove of cottonwood, elm, and box elder. He pulled his tobacco sack and papers from his pocket to roll a cigarette.

Sunlight shimmered from a gun barrel. In the tall grass. Far side of the creek. Twenty yards downstream. He was edgy without appearing to be, continuing to crease the paper for the tobacco and letting his horse walk. From under his pulled-down hat, he could see the dark shape of a rifleman lying in the buffalo grass. Waiting. There was no time to wonder why.

The man was expecting Checker to ride unsuspectingly along the creek and pass right in front of his position on the opposite side. If the ranger turned around now, his back would be a big inviting target. In one continuous movement, Checker spurred his horse into a run along the creek line toward the ambusher, dropped the sack and papers, swung to the right side of his horse to hide himself and pulled his pistol.

A rifle shot cracked into the empty air where he had been moments before. Then another. Checker snapped a shot under his horse's neck as he galloped past the hidden rifleman. After passing, Checker sat upright and spun his charging horse toward the creek bed itself. Grass blades whipped his chaps as he jumped the stream and disappeared into the heavy trees alongside it. A rifle shot spit into the water behind him.

The ambusher turned to track Checker's flanking movement behind the front line of the grove. The ranger flashed momentarily from behind each advancing tree as he sped through the woods toward his would-be assassin. The bearded outlaw fired twice, tearing into tree limbs and trunks.

Like a roaring train, Checker crashed into the open, directly in line with the startled rifleman. The ranger's Colt exploded three times as his big horse thundered toward the ambusher. A rifle bullet whizzed past Checker's head.

The man's rifle dropped as he froze, held stangely in place by the impact of Checker's bullets. Then the invisible wall gave way and he fell face foward into the mud. His upper body rose once like a man about to do a push-up, then collapsed. A red pool began to seep into the soggy earth under him.

Pulling his horse into a stutter-step, Checker spun the animal around and re-entered the dark of the trees. But slowly this time. He trotted forward, staying within the wooded cover, to see if any more ambushers lay ahead. His caution was rewarded. Two men on horseback were waiting fifty yards away, where the trail entered an opening between the ridge and a grassy hill. Backups for the first rifleman.

This was no casual robbery. These men were waiting to kill him. Right now both men were standing in their stirrups, apparently waiting to see if their comrade had completed the task. These men had known he was at Amelia's house! Had someone followed him from camp? Was he too distracted about seeing her to pay attention? He didn't think so. But these men had been waiting for him. Far enough away from the Hedricksons so there would be no witnesses—and no help.

The former ranger shoved his pistol into its holster and pulled the Winchester from its boot. Checker eased his big horse forward, through the dark treeline, trying to get as close as he could before being seen. He would try to disarm them and find some answers.

The taller of the two men caught the movement within the trees and realized its significance. Without a word, he yanked his horse around and spurred hard. The second man followed. Checker ordered them to stop and fired once, a warning shot over their heads. He had never shot a man in the back and didn't intend to start now. If there was any hesitation on their part, it was unseen by the ranger. The two outlaws disappeared quickly over a ridge.

Ignoring their flight, Checker kicked his own horse into a run directly for the Triple C camp. More important than catching up with the two ambushers, he needed to reach the bedground and be sure everything was all right. His friends should be well on the way to town by now, but he had a bad feeling this attempted ambush was connected to the herd. It made no sense otherwise.

Twenty minutes later, a riderless horse came into view as he cleared a ravine and the last half mile to camp. The horse was grazing. A man lay beside the quiet animal. Checker slowed his own mount to a walk so it wouldn't frighten the other horse as they approached. The grazing bay was without a saddle; a hastily-tied rope halter was tangling from its nose to the ground.

Approaching carefully, the ranger soon realized the downed man was Randy Reilman, the Triple C wrangler. Reilman was in his long johns and boots. No hat. A Winchester was under him. Pulling up beside him, Checker jumped from his saddle, held the reins, and kneeled beside the wrangler.

Turning him over slowly, Checker saw a blood-crusted crease alongside Reilman's forehead where a bullet had nearly ended his life. The wrangler was alive but barely conscious. Water from Checker's canteen brought Reilman around. The wounded cowboy focused his eyes for the first time.

"Checker . . . that you, Checker?"

"Yeah, it's me. What happened, Randy?"

"Ambushed . . . surrounded . . . sleeping," the wrangler swallowed and tried to form the words. "Saw Seals at the remuda . . . Goddamn guns tore into us . . . scared our hosses . . . Caught my bay . . . I . . . goddamn."

Checker had wrapped the man's bloody head with his

rolled-up kerchief. Reilman continued to talk, almost jab-ber. His ramblings about horses slowly began to take focus. He recounted the night's horror more precisely but still didn't remember anything after getting on his horse. Ob-viously, the bullet alongside his head had knocked him out.

Finally, with Reilman's assurance that he was able to stand, Checker eventually got him into his saddle. They started toward the camp, riding double, on Checker's big horse. Reilman's bay allowed the ranger to adjust the rope halter enough so he could lead the animal as they traveled.

The wounded Reilman sagged into sleep, weak with shock and loss of blood. Checker held him in place as they rode. Eight longhorns, all carrying the Triple C brand, me-andered in front as they moved toward the camp. The ranger's hard eyes searched for signs of riders. But the plains were empty, except for a band of scruffy-looking buffalo and a coyote that followed them for a half hour. He was certain they weren't being trailed.

At the Triple C camp, three of the night guards stood, watching him come in. They had arrived only a few min-utes earlier. Their rifles were lowered as soon as they real-ized who was headed toward them. Disbelief and despair were the only stories their faces told. The ranger realized what had happened. The impact of seeing the emptied bedground was numbing even to his battle-hardened mind.

Jackson and Harry Clanahan greeted Checker and helped Reilman out of the saddle. The Irishman was limp-ing. The third nighthawk, Tex, was lying under a tree, cov-ered by a blanket. Jackson had worked on his broken leg; two sticks were wrapped in place on each side to keep the limb straight. A purple welt anchored his forehead.

Weak from shock and pain, Tex managed to sit up and said, "Hello, ranger. Where you been? We done run into hell."

The tall ranger leaned over and put his hand on Tex's

good shoulder. Checker reached for words of comfort, "Glad to see you made it, Tex. You rest easy now."

"Meanin' no disrespect . . . but I don't think any of us ever will again," Tex said.

Checker didn't respond, except to step back and help Jackson and Clanahan ease Reilman alongside Tex. They gave him some water and laid another blanket across him. The wrangler quickly went to sleep.

The ranger's mind recounted the men missing from the woeful scene. The names that hit him hardest were Dan Mitchell, Jake Woodman, Sonny Jones, Tug, and Tyrel Bannon. It was hard to believe they were dead. He shook his head and tried to concentrate on what they should do next. Anger was filling his soul.

Jackson described what had happened, then pointed out the fresh grave. He figured somebody was still alive and had driven the wagon to town. And likely, another hand was wounded and in the wagon or the other man wouldn't have used it in the first place. They walked to the wagon ruts leaving the camp, then to the rock-covered mounds.

The black man continued, "John, somebody showed serious gumption to hitch up trail horses like that."

"Aye, he did the burying first, bless him. Maybe there be more than two. Saints be praised, if that's a truth," Clanahan observed, "Wonder who it is."

Jackson told Checker one nighthawk was dead, Freddie Tucker. But no one knew whether the other two nighthawks, Sonny Jones and Tyrel Bannon, had made it. And they had no idea of where to look for the herd. Or what they should do next. Clanahan mentioned returning to Texas. Tex wondered if they should dig up the grave to find out who was there.

Their sense of defeat was complete. Their friends were dead or unaccounted for. The frustration of not even knowing who was alive was almost as heavy a blow as the destruction itself. Their long challenge to bring a herd to

Dodge City had been destroyed. Before anyone realized it, there was silence. No one was speaking. They were looking at John Checker. He understood they were expecting him to tell them what to do.

"Damn, boys, this one's hard to swallow," the ranger said. He shoved his hat back on his head and his dark hair rippled against his shoulders. Nods of agreement followed. Clanahan spat a long Irish curse. Jackson turned away briefly and rubbed his eyes. Tex stared at the ground.

"That all you got to say?" Tex asked, not bothering to look up, frustration and pain heating his words. "Hell, Mitchell hired you for your gun. We're just cowpunchers. You weren't even here when they came at us."

Jackson exploded, "That's the stupidest thing I've ever heard, Tex! You haven't got the brains God gave—"

"That's all right, Jackson. I know how he feels. I wish I'd been here, too," Checker responded.

Clanahan threw his arms in the air and exclaimed, "I say we be leaving this bleeming Kansas—and leave it to the devil. The sweet earth of Texas is calling."

Checker listened before continuing. Tex's words had struck the opened wound of guilt. He should have been here, his mind kept repeating. He fought back the same feelings the Irishman had, of wanting to ride away from this awful place of death and never return. But he had done that before, a long time ago. He wasn't leaving his time.

"I'm not running. You can if you want . . . and no hard feelings. I'm going to find out who did this, get our herd back, and make 'em pay," he stated, catching the eyes of each man as he delivered the promise. The words rolled out of his mouth without any conscious decision to say them. Jackson instantly gave his support; Clanahan's was a heartbeat behind.

"Hell, it was a goddamn war party. How we gonna find 'em—or fight 'em—with just us?" Tex asked sarcastically.

"I'd bet a lot it wasn't Indians," Checker declared. "Three men tried to bushwhack me coming from my sister's place. I don't think it was road agents who happened by."

"What happened?" Tex asked, wide-eyed and leaning forward.

"One won't bother anybody anymore. The other two got away," the tall ranger reported.

Tex's eyes went involuntarily to Checker's reverse-draw holster holding the short-barreled Colt .45 with the black handles and the half-cut-away trigger guard, then to the ranger's Comanche tunic and the arrowhead scar on the ranger's cheek.

Jackson caught the more significant message, "You figure it was rustlers, leaving signs to throw everybody off?"

"Yeah, I do and—" Checker stopped in midsentence and pointed to the tiny blur of a rider coming toward them from the north.

"Grab your guns, boys, they're comin' again," Tex hollered from his resting spot. His yell woke Reilman, who sat straight up, disoriented.

"No . . . no . . . it's Sonny," Checker responded.

"Yeah, that's Sonny," Jackson said, "but that ain't the horse he was ridin'."

Clanahan calmed Reilman back into his resting position. In a few minutes, the happy cowboy with the outlaw past reined up on a lathered bay and hopped down. His shirt was mud-streaked and torn in places. Jackson grabbed the reins and handed Sonny a canteen. He took a long swallow, then another, wiped his mouth on his ripped shirt sleeve, and reported.

"Found the herd! Big open valley. Cut by a long stream. Maybe three miles from here. North," Sonny exclaimed, taking off his hat and holding it in one hand and wiping his forehead with the same sleeve. He told of trailing the rustlers after catching a second horse.

"Fifteen men . . . moving 'em hard to Dodge. Ain't no

more than a handful of hours away from there now. They'll hit town before dusk easy." He continued, "Boys, here's the worst side of it, I reckon. Seals was with 'em. He's part of the gang."

The response was silence, trailed by coarse threats of what they would do to Seals when he was caught.

"I saw a fella ride up. Town man, I reckon. Short hombre in a fancy gray suit. Like one of them banker fellas. From the looks of it, he was calling the shots. He talked with Seals and some other ranny."

"Well done, my friend," Checker responded.

Without speaking, Checker went over to the burned-out chuck wagon. The others watched as he removed burned gear and clothes. Finally he turned back around, "Suspected as much. The trail box is gone."

"Seals," Jackson replied.

"Yeah," Checker agreed. "From what Randy told me, Seals must've cut loose the horses too."

"Didn't leave much to chance, did they?" the black man mused. Ceremoniously, he pulled a scratched pipe from his vest, fingered loose tobacco into the bowl from a small leather bag, and packed it with his forefinger. As he prepared the pipe, Jackson explained they had rounded up six horses on the way back but hadn't found any more Triple C riders or cattle.

A match's flame was drawn to the tobacco, creating a soft string of smoke. Jackson's forehead furrowed with worry.

"If there's a townie involved, that means whoever went to town is in danger," the black man said.

Checker didn't answer.

"You think they be coming our way once more?" Clanahan asked, his hand involuntarily resting on the butt of his pistol.

"Anybody's guess, I reckon," Checker answered. "Mine is they want that herd in and sold before any questions are asked. Then they'll scatter and no one's the wiser. They count on us being dead, or running away—or real slow coming to town.

"Here's my thinking. See how it tracks with you, boys. I'll ride hard for town. You boys get something to eat. Then, Sonny, you lead everybody back to the herd. Follow 'em, but not close. Stay out of sight. Don't take any chances."

"I can ride, dammit!" Tex yelled. "Jes' git me on top of a cayuse."

"Counting on it, Tex," Checker said, without looking at the wounded cowboy.

"What's your play, John?" Sonny asked.

Checker intended to round up some Texas cowboys in town to help. Shanghai Pierce, in particular, owed him a favor. Together, they would ride back to meet the herd. The five Triple C riders would come up from the rear and cut off any escape.

"You gonna look for . . . the Triple C boys?" Jackson asked, his pipe tight in his mouth.

"Right away," Checker answered.

"What if they aren't there?" Jackson followed.

"Got a hunch they'll get through. No one will be looking for a wagon, to begin with," Checker responded as positively as possible, "but I won't be able to spend much time searching. There isn't time. We need to stop those thieving murderers before they bring the herd in."

Sonny's eyes narrowed, then he began unsaddling his lathered horse, "I'm ready . . . but I'd better switch hosses. This ol' boy is done played out. If we see that townie headed back, should we take him?"

"Your call, Sonny. But I doubt he'll stay around long," the former ranger said, lifting the stirrup flap to check on his own cinch. "I intend to find him—in Dodge."

Jackson was sorting through the various sacks of apples, potatoes, and beans near the chuck wagon. In one hand, he held one of the slabs of salt pork; in the other, a black skillet. Checker handed Clanahan his saddlebags filled with food his sister had insisted he take.

"Well, all I can tell you is he's short, sorta skinny. Yellow haired. Had a gray suit, like I said. Fancy hat to match. Oh yeah, he rode a sorrel with one white stocking. Right foreleg. Flashy lookin' hoss, that's for sure," Sonny advised, lifting his saddle off the tired animal.

"That'll help. You'd make a good lawman, Jones," Checker said and grinned.

The cowboy laughed, stood the saddle upright on the ground with the mantle down, and said, "Sounds good to me. I just want first crack at Seals."

"First, bejesus! You'll have to wait behind this Irishman!" Clanahan bantered as he carefully laid out the ranger's packed sandwiches, apples, and a jar of peach preserves on the ground.

"We're gonna need some more leather," Jackson advised. "I wonder where the rest of the tack is?"

"And the rest of the hardware," Sonny said suddenly. "Then let's git at the eatin'. My belly's done figured I forgot it was down there!"

At the same moment, each man remembered the missing cook. Coughs tried to fill the awkward silence. Tex slowly stood, shaking off Clanahan's offer to help. The handsome cowboy's star-studded chaps were smeared with dried mud and blood. Grimacing, he spoke through his teeth, "Ranger, you really think we can do this?"

Checker swung up onto his black, looked at the wounded man, and answered, "I aim to try. And I can't think of any men I'd rather be tryin' it with."

"What if you don't come?" Tex asked.

"If I don't come it's because I'm dead," Checker answered with no emotion in his voice. He nudged the big horse with his spurs and was into a full run in three strides.

Sonny was the first to speak, "Honest to God, I think I

feel sorry for those rustler bastards. John Checker is like having hell chasing you."

Jackson laughed and reinforced the point with a simple "Amen."

"You think he's that good?" Tex shrugged his shoulders as he spoke.

Sonny looked scornfully at the cowboy. "If you knew how good, Tex, you'd be shakin' . . . after the stupid things you said to him earlier."

The growing thunder of advancing cattle swallowed the tiny song of a nearby bobolink. Alongside a thicket of blackjack, Star McCallister sat atop his sorrel and liked what he saw. A sea of Triple C cattle was moving toward him, headed for Dodge City, guided by his men.

He pulled a cigar from the inside pocket of his suit coat and lit it with a match struck across his saddle horn. His face and hair were illuminated by the flame. White smoke wound along the curled, short brim of his cocked hat and escaped into the sky. As he moved, the pearl-handled pistol in a shoulder holster was for a brief moment visible under his jacket.

After a few puffs, he waved at the two front riders and they quickly responded by galloping toward him. One was Henry Seals. The other was a snake-faced man with large pale eyes, called Waco. Like his boss, Waco had a shoulder holster under his left armpit. Only Waco's was visible, strapped over a red shirt. Stuck in his waistband was a second pistol.

"What do you think, Star? We did all right, didn't we?" Seals asked, smiling widely and seeking approval as they reined up in front of the gang leader. Waco glanced at Seals contemptuously, then back at McCallister.

"Yeah, after I shoved some guts up your ass," Star snapped.

Seals's smile disappeared as fast as it had come. Without further comment, McCallister briefed them on what he expected from this point foward, reviewing the details he felt important.

He told Seals to hold the herd at the Arkansas, on the south side of the river, where grazing was plentiful. When the herd was settled there, Seals would come across, acting as the trail boss. As soon as the buy was completed, Seals would return and the cattle would then be moved across the toll bridge and into the stockyards.

Having the herd in town for the shortest time possible was the saloon keeper's goal, as always. If they were lucky, the animals might be moved directly into railroad cars and gone before nightfall. McCallister would quietly see what timing could be arranged. Nothing overt on his part, however.

But with so many trains carrying beef, it usually wasn't hard to determine the best movement. No gang member, especially Seals, was to remain in town after the herd was delivered. They were to return immediately to the main hideout. Waco would bring cash and whiskey to celebrate.

Seals was to check in with McCallister first at the Nueces, before going to the buyer, in case there was a change in plans. A new account at the Mercantile had been opened under the name "3C Company." The money would be moved on to a Wichita bank the next day. McCallister would advise Seals on the details of the initial deposit when it was appropriate.

McCallister asked to see the Triple C trail papers. Seals took them from inside his shirt, apologizing for the dampness from his sweat. Waco shook his head and rolled a cigarette.

McCallister returned them and said, "Nathan Wilson is the man you want to see. He's buying the herd. Government man. Indian affairs. He'll ask for a thousand dollars. Under the table. That's his standard fee. Give it to him."

"Where will I find this Nathan Wilson, Star?" Seals asked.

"Most likely at the Long Branch. If not, he'll be at his office—over the Wright store. You can't miss the place," McCallister continued, "but you come to the Nueces first—to see me. Remember, act like you don't know me. You got that?"

Waco motioned for the gang to keep the herd moving past them as McCallister rehearsed Seals on what to say and do when he met the buyer. Waco was to go with the saloon keeper now into town, along with two other men— just in case any Triple C riders showed up before the deal was completed. The snake-eyed man's pale eyes glittered with anticipation upon hearing the news.

"I thought they were all dead!" Seals exclaimed.

"How the hell would we know that?" Waco snapped. "It was dark, you idiot. That's why we always spread around the damn Injun stuff. Sends 'em off for the army—if'n they go anywhere."

McCallister's eyes fluttered, then stopped. He drew on his cigar and said coldly, "If anyone gets to town, we'll handle it."

Waco grinned. "Damn, you're jumpy, Seals. Can't be more than three or four of 'em left. They're rubbing their heads—or running for Texas so fast they've got their hosses' tails up their butts. Hell, we walked around the whole damn camp. I didn't see nobody alive."

Seals tried to look reassured and shrugged. Waco followed up his remarks by asking McCallister if he wanted to send some men to see if any Triple C men had made it.

McCallister's response was terse. "No. Keep the men here moving beef. Time is too important to waste it counting bodies."

"What about Checker?" Seals blurted out.

"Checker's dead. I sent three men to kill him after he

left his sister's house," McCallister reported, growing impatient with the cowboy's questions.

"Sister?! Checker's got a sister around here?! How'd you know that?" Seals said in wonderment.

"There are a lot of things you don't know, Seals," McCallister responded. "All that matters is Checker's dead."

Waco's laugh was long and shrill, like a horse neighing before a fight.

"Come on, Waco, let's go. Bring Iron and Ferguson. I'll see you in town, Seals," McCallister said, swinging his sorrel to the north. "Remember, you come to me first—but you don't know me."

CHAPTER 9

"WELL, BOSS, WE'RE here."

Without turning from his driver's seat on the calf wagon, Tyrel Bannon spoke to the wounded Dan Mitchell lying on the planked bed. Tug was chattering to himself from his seat beside the young rider. They were entering the major intersection of Dodge City, Front and Bridge Streets.

Immediately behind was the toll bridge across the Arkansas River. His sun-wrinkled face etched in pain, Mitchell was sleeping or had been when the young rider last looked. Bannon's and Mitchell's saddles were in the wagon bed along with the wounded trail boss. They'd been moving since false dawn.

Several times, the farm boy had imagined what it was going to be like when the Triple C herd crossed: a long brown stream cutting through a wide blue river. Instead, the Triple C consisted of a creaky wagon that had once held trail calves, a bloody trail boss, a cranky cook, and a greenhorn.

Ahead were the railroad tracks connecting this wild place on the windy plains to the cities of the east. Ahead were more false-front buildings, shanties, saloons, noise, and people than the farm boy had ever seen in his life—or ever thought existed.

It was absolutely stunning. Even his friends' blustery campfire descriptions had been inadequate, as overblown as they had seemed at the time. For nearly three months, he'd seen nothing but cattle, cowboys, land, sky, and rivers.

Now this, this Babylon of color, noise, and activity engulfed the wagon unmercifully.

Panic seized him. So many people! He wanted to turn back. The young rider clenched his fists and bit the inside of his cheeks, hoping the pain would bring the strength to stay and not run. Tug noticed his nervousness and asked if the boy was ill. Bannon said nothing, fighting to control his fear.

A tobacco-spitting driver of a passing freighter cursed him for stopping.

Bannon gulped in long, deep breaths, craving the air and its delivered calm. With renewed resolve, he scanned the busy Front Street area for some clue to where a doctor might be found. Finally Bannon told the feisty cook that he was fine.

On the north side of Front Street—the "deadline" that Harry Clanahan told about—the respectable community stretched for at least eight blocks. It was another world from just this morning when he had ridden through the prairie, seeing the ravaged remains of dead Triple C steers, calves, and horses dotting the land.

Worse was coming upon what was left of Freddie Tucker and one body Bannon didn't recognize. He would have known Tucker's faded red shirt anywhere; it might have been the only one the cowboy owned. Little else of the man was left. Bannon had lost what little breakfast he had eaten.

Coyotes and vultures had ripped away the humanness, leaving merely bits of clothing and weapons for identification. Captain had driven off the ugly birds with a vengeance that matched the anger swelling within the young rider.

At Tug's insistence, he had buried the remains of their comrade in a shallow grave next to a cluster of windblown trees. The other body was near the dry creek bed, lying among clumps of tall buffalo grass. He wouldn't have seen it except for the coyote tearing on a rib cage. The clothing certainly wasn't anything he remembered any of the missing Triple C riders wearing, so it must've been one of the rustlers.

Tug agreed with Bannon to leave the remains where they were. If their friends had killed any other ambushers, they must have been carried off, simply missing this one. Tug said it could stay there forever for all he cared, and leave those remains. Bannon agreed, but chose not to demonstrate his feelings.

The young rider reined in the two wagon horses to let a fancy buggy cross in front of them. The streets were streaming with crisscrossing horses, wagons, and carriages. A hay wagon went by on his left, spewing loose golden strands as it banged along. Another wagon came out of a side street and pulled in behind Bannon, following his course for a block, before turning off. Freighters were everywhere; their drivers' coarse yells and crisp bullwhips created a weird song, distinctive from the other city noises. Tug yelled back a few colorful phrases to make up for the younger man's silent intimidation.

Over and over to himself, Bannon kept hoping the sorrel and Sonny's brown didn't decide to act up. Strangers might wonder what kind of a fool would hitch two trail broncs to a wagon in the first place. Neither animal cared much for the pulling nor understood well what they were supposed to be doing.

The trip to town had taken twice as long as it should have. Bannon had spent much of it yanking, yelling, and coaxing them into some semblance of a team. Not many horses take right off to pulling a wagon. And he had been luckier than anyone had a right to be. Tug kept telling him that. Still, he wished for their cooperation, especially now that they were in the big city where everyone would be watching.

The third horse, the reluctant bay, had finally decided

to come along too. It was tied to the back of the wagon on a lead rope. Nothing about being pulled along by the wagon was a happy experience for the animal. The bay whinnied to the other two, dug in its heels when the wagon slowed, and shook its thick neck wildly at every opportunity. Captain, the trail boss's three-legged dog, trotted comfortably beside the right front wheel.

Bannon clucked to the horses and headed along the colorful assembly of saloons, dance halls, dining places, hotels, and gambling houses. Finding a doctor was his only objective, but his eyes were drawn, in wonderment, to the endless string of colorful signs. He passed the Alamo, Long Branch, Billiard Hall, Alhambra, Saratoga, Occident, Nueces, Crystal Palace, Old House, Hub, Sample Room, Oasis, and the Junction. A woman waved from an upper window. Right friendly, he thought. Tug elbowed Bannon and grinned. The farm boy's face reddened.

"They sure do like Texans here, it appears, Tug," he said to the smiling cook. "See there. Lone Star. A fine place, I reckon."

The bald-headed cook agreed, "It sure do appear that way, son."

Everybody was either busy, drunk, or having fun. Cowboys lined the wooden sidewalks, some of them Mexicans shouting out words to Spanish songs. A mustached cowboy was playing his harmonica as an appreciative crowd gave him raucous encouragement. Bannon thought he saw the faces of Sonny Jones and Tex among them and stared intensely into the half circle milling around the performer outside the Nueces. Nausea followed as he realized the foolishness of his thought.

As special attractions to join the activities inside, women with heavy rouge and bright dresses stood outside some of the places. Bannon was fascinated by each one, whether she was pretty or not. It had been a long time since he had even seen a woman. One lady smiled and winked at the young rider as he rode by. That made him feel welcome, even if it was for the wrong reasons. Tug quickly advised him that she was winking at him. Bannon acknowledged that this was probably true.

But to himself, the young man recalled his mother getting upset when a widow once said he was a "handsome sight." Maybe he'd tell her another lady was after him. The thought made him chuckle.

Cowboys strolled the street in their finest garb, jingling spurs, new hats, and even new three-piece suits—and wide grins. Some looked like drinking had taken away their trail sense for the moment. But it was easy to see why, Bannon observed, with all these inviting places to go to after so long a time without any comforts.

Suddenly resentment flowed into Bannon's mind, resentment that anyone could be having fun at a time like this. No one should be laughing or singing. Or dancing. This was a terrible time and all should be abiding by the gloom he felt. But a glance back at the sleeping Mitchell made him realize there was no time for sightseeing or feeling sorry for himself. They needed a doctor. Pulling up to the closest hitching rail, he questioned a dour storekeeper and was told the directions to a Doctor Tremons's house. The man said the physician was known to treat cowboys on occasion, implying that no respectable medical practitioner in Dodge City would want to care for a Texas drover.

Returning to the wagon, Bannon said, "Tug, there's a doc on the other side of town. I can find it, I reckon."

"Sure you can, son. Sure you can."

Bannon snapped the reins and called out to the two horses to move on. Sonny's brown stepped out as the dominant horse. They passed more saloons and gambling houses. The railroad depot and nearby water tank were impressive to view for a young man who'd never seen a train before. A few blocks to the east, they could make out the city's mammoth cattle pens and loading yard, filled with thousands of animals. They passed merchants of all kinds: a barbershop, clothing store, boot maker, gunsmith, drug store, and saddle maker.

At the corner of Bridge Avenue and Front Street, as they left the south side of Dodge, was the Wright, Beverly & Company general store. Tug observed, "That thar store has nigh onto everything a man could ever want, Ty. Clothes an' groceries an' saddles, guns, every kind of hardware, knives, tobaccy, an' wagons even. Hear tell they got a portable house for sale, Ty. Yesiree. We should go in an' see our'n self."

"Well, that's real nice, Tug. Maybe we can come back some time. After we get Dan to this Doctor Tremons," Bannon replied, letting his frustration bite into the words. Tug looked at him, surprised and a little hurt.

A half hour later, Bannon and Tug pulled up in front of Dr. Howard Tremons's small frame house in the residential section of Dodge City. As Bannon jumped out of the wagon, the doctor himself came out of the door, more from curiosity than purpose.

Dr. Tremons was a tall man with spectacles, graying hair, and a thin mustache. He walked with a slight limp.

"Get him inside. He's lost too much blood," Dr. Tremons ordered after a quick glance at the unconscious Mitchell.

"You betcha, Doc," Tug said.

Bannon replied, "I've got money to pay."

"No need to insult me, son."

"Didn't mean it that way, I—"

"I'm sure you didn't. What happened?"

Before Bannon could speak further, Tug told the story in a handful of colorful sentences as the three men carried the half-conscious Mitchell toward the house. The young rider told Captain to stay with the horses and was proud the dog obeyed.

The trail boss awakened as they neared the doorway and said, "Wha-a . . . let me down! I can walk! Dammit, I'm . . ."

The three men responded to his urging and let him down. Mitchell gamely wobbled to an upright position, then collapsed.

"Get him!" ordered the doctor. Bannon grabbed the trail boss under the shoulders and kept him from hitting the ground. There was no argument from Mitchell as they lifted him again, only nonsensical phrases from the foreman about the herd being bogged down in quicksand and no one having any ladders.

Once in his office, Dr. Tremons helped Bannon and Tug put the wounded man on a low-standing table. Washed clean, it was centered in a cramped room lined with cabinets and counters and cluttered with bottles and shiny instruments of various shapes and sizes.

With no wasted motion, the doctor grabbed a large, green-glass bottle, poured some of its liquid in a cloth, and placed it over Mitchell's mouth and nose. He was soon unconscious.

"I-i-is he alive?" the young rider exclaimed in fearful response to the sudden change.

"Chloroform. Knocks 'em out. Makes surgery easier for him—and me. He'll come awake in an hour. I know what I'm doing," the doctor said.

"Didn't mean to sound like I was worried, Doc. Just haven't been around many doctors. Never seen one before, actually. He's my friend and—"

"This bullet isn't going to kill him, son. He's a tough old rascal."

Tug was soon engrossed in the medical procedures. Bannon didn't want to watch, but he did. What was left of Mitchell's shirt was cut away, then his shirt-sleeve bandages.

"Well, son, now we know why you've a liking for one-armed shirts," Dr. Tremons said, smiling. Bannon blushed and rubbed his bared arm with the other. When the doctor saw the moss, the farm boy had a sick feeling the physician was going to be angry. Instead, he nodded.

"Where'd you learn this?" Dr. Tremons said without looking up.

"From him."

"Smart man."

Just before operating, the doctor paused and invited the young rider to move away from the table. "Tyrel, there's hot coffee right around the corner. In the kitchen. There. Cups should be handy, too. Why don't you get yourself some while ol' Tug and I handle this."

Bannon was eager to follow his suggestion. He returned after the bullet had been removed and real bandages were in place. Pasting a stray hair lock in place with his fingers, Dr. Tremons said again that Dan Mitchell would make it just fine but he needed sleep, time to heal.

"He'll need to stay here a few days. But he'll be just fine. I bet you men could use a drink."

The tall doctor brought out a bottle of whiskey and three glasses. They sat and talked for a while. Bannon and Tug told him more about the trail drive and the ambush. The doctor spoke about Dodge and his own life.

Dr. Tremon's stiffened left leg was a personal reminder of the War between the States. The reason for that condition the doctor was quick to share: Confederate rifle fire had hit him twice on the Little Roundtop at Gettysburg. But if Dr. Tremons had any problem helping a Texas cowboy, it didn't show.

The doctor invited both men to stay for supper. His daughter would be home soon and she would enjoy the company too. Father and daughter lived alone; Sarah Ann helped as a nurse. Today she was out buying supplies. Mrs. Tremons had died several years earlier from the fevers. The doctor told the story, adding sidelights about his wife and swallowing several times to keep back emotion.

Tug eagerly accepted but Bannon declined, saying he needed to talk with the town marshal.

"You know, son, most people think the law is supposed to protect us townfolks from Texas cowboys like you. Not for watching over Texas herds comin' in."

Bannon opened his mouth to respond, but the doctor continued, "Since this shootout involved Indians, it's likely the army is your only bet for help. But I doubt them blue-bellies'll go ridin' after your beef, son."

"Thanks, Doc. But I need to try."

"I understand, son. Hope I'm wrong. Bastards that would do a thing like this need to be hauled to justice."

"Tyrel, we could eat and then go see the sheriff. An' maybe that Wright store too," Tug said, downing his second glassful of whiskey in one long swallow.

"If the doc doesn't mind, I like the idea of your stayin' here with the boss. But I need to do this . . . now," the young rider said.

Tug looked sheepishly at Bannon, "You don't mind if I stay here then?"

"Oh, no, that's good, Tug. I'll be back later."

Bannon shook the doctor's hand and said, "Thank you, Doc, for everything. We owe you a lot."

At the young rider's request, Dr. Tremons told him where to find the marshal's office. Bannon stood beside Mitchell for a moment before leaving.

"Cowboy, I don't know what you're looking for . . . but you're going to find a .45 slug in your belly if you don't put that shotgun down. Right now." That was Tyrel Bannon's greeting from Dodge City Marshal Jubal Rand as the young rider entered the marshal's office. Right then, Bannon realized walking in holding a gun wasn't very smart. But bringing Tug's shotgun from the wagon outside had felt comforting. Especially in a town so big and bewildering.

"Sorry, sir, didn't mean no harm," Bannon answered and looked for a place to lay it down quickly. Facing him ten feet away was a cocked Colt Peacemaker held by a narrow-faced man with a handlebar mustache, closely cropped hair, and a sour manner. His clothes were those of a businessman, only his coat was off, thrown casually over a chair in the corner of the room. His fancy white shirt was obviously one of style. A star glittered from his unbuttoned vest.

On the desk was a worn deck of cards, spread out in a game of solitaire, and a stack of different-sized papers. It was midday, but one would be hard-pressed to know it in the cramped room. Oily, sallow light from two wall lamps were no match for sunshine. Off to the left, six cells were occupied by sleeping men. Their snoring ripped into the main room at regular intervals.

Marshal Rand casually explained the jailed men. "A bunch of Shanghai Pierce's boys got into it with some Mexicans. Me an' my deputies had to take the starch out of 'em."

He paused and gave what must have been his idea of a grin, then added, "Them Mexs are a cruel bunch, with a likin' for knives. Don't reckon you Texas boys care much for the way they handle hosses neither."

Bannon nodded respectfully. He couldn't remember meeting any Mexicans but didn't want to act naive. Over on the far wall was a rack of rifles and two shotguns. A pot of coffee was boiling on a black stove in the corner. It looked good to Bannon, but he didn't think he should ask for some.

"What do you want, boy?" The question snapped like a pistol shot, as the rawboned lawman casually disengaged the hammer and let the handle slide downward in his hand so the barrel pointed to the ceiling. He laid the gun over the forgotten cards and stared at the young rider.

"Just got in town," Bannon said, unnerved by the lawman's curt style. "We . . . I . . . we are the Triple C, outta Texas—"

"That's obvious. You Texas boys look alike."

"Got ambushed. Herd stolen." The young rider thrust his chin forward in silent defiance of the remark. He'd never talked to a peace officer before and this one was an intimidating man, to boot.

"Crew was killed. All except me, our cook, and our trail boss. I just left him—my boss—with the doc. Our cook stayed there with him. Our herd was run off. Reckon it was redskins. Figured the law would want to know about this right away."

"Where'd this supposedly happen?"

Bannon ignored the "supposedly" and answered, "About five miles south of here. Nice piece of flat grazin'. Been holding 'em—"

"Yeah, I know about where you're talking."

The marshal followed that by asking if Bannon's herd had wandered onto any farm land. The young rider assured him they had not. Nervously, Bannon shifted his weight from one foot to the other as he told his story. It was hard to tell if the lawman was listening or not. Rand's slate-colored eyes wandered to the papers. He leafed through them as the young rider spoke, silently evaluating their contents, making it rudely clear that his interest in Bannon's story was minimal.

"So . . . I'll be ready to lead the posse any time you are," Bannon finished.

"Posse?"

"Well, sir, that may not be what you call it here . . . in Kansas," the young rider said, fighting the irritation welling within him. "I just meant . . . I want to ride with you—or whoever goes after those savages."

"How many trail drives you been on, boy?" The cynical lawman grinned.

"This is my first."

Conversation stopped while Marshal Rand bit off the end of a dark cigar, pulled a match from his vest, and popped it to life on the buckle of his gun belt. White smoke wandered toward Tyrel Bannon. Bannon wondered if that was the end of the discussion.

"That's rough country you boys came through. I know of three herds lost to the rivers, for sure. Half of it's Indian land to begin with. Now, you're asking me to go looking for some redskins with a herd of beef out there?" he asked, without looking up. "Hell, by now, they've eaten it, run it off, or killed it."

"What do you usually do when somebody kills a bunch of people and takes their cattle?" Bannon's response had a mean edge. Rand wasn't what he'd expected. He was supposed to be angry that honest men had been murdered and jump to help find the culprits that did it.

"Texas, I don't know who you are. Never heard of the Triple C. An' me an' my deputies aren't about to go running out anywhere on some greenhorn's word. Ride on back to Texas, boy. While you can."

Bannon couldn't help himself and blurted, "So you don't care what happened to my friends?"

He was looking straight into Rand's impenetrable eyes. Visually, no quarter was asked; none given in return.

Exasperated at the cowboy's reaction, Rand stood, both his hands on the desk. Three papers flew onto the floor. He looked straight at Bannon and said, "Dammit, boy! We don't have Indian trouble around here. It's only you cowboys that seem to get 'em riled up. If it was up to me, I'd get rid of all of them red bastards."

Bannon's eyes slowly moved to gaze at the floor and his worn boots. The lawman thought for a moment, then said, "You've got an army matter, boy. Your best bet is to head for the fort west of here. Fort Dodge. Maybe they'll send out a patrol. Most likely, though, they won't . . ."

Marshal Rand was distracted as the door opened behind Bannon. The young man turned his head toward the interruption. A small, blondish man with a thin face and deep-set eyes entered. His gray suit and matching hat were streaked with trail dust.

"Afternoon, Star, what can I do for you?" the lawman welcomed.

"Oh, I'm sorry, Marshal Rand . . . and you, young man . . . didn't realize you were busy," Star McCallister replied, reaching for the doorknob. "I was just going to check to see if you expected any more trouble tonight."

"No, no, that's all right. This cowboy was just leaving."

Bannon was annoyed even more; it had to be obvious to this man that someone was with the marshal, yet he chose to come in anyway. Was everyone rude in Dodge, except Dr. Tremons?

Star McCallister smiled and asked, "Young man, please forgive my forwardness, but, by the looks of your shirt, it appears you've had some difficulty."

Before Bannon could respond, the marshal told the saloon owner of the young rider's plight. McCallister's forehead creased into a frown.

"I heard some Indians were off the reservation," Star said, his eyelids fluttering. "Are you the only survivor, son?"

Bannon was taken by the businessman's apparent concern. Silently, he criticized himself for being so quick with his judgment of the man's manners. Pulling lightly on his earlobe, the young rider explained how he and the cook had brought their badly wounded trail boss to Dr. Tremons and that the other Triple C men were dead. As he spoke, McCallister walked over to the stove, poured two cups of coffee without asking the marshal's permission, and returned.

"I'm very sorry to hear this. I'd be pleased to treat you

and your friend to dinner at my place. The Nueces. Just down the street," McCallister said and handed one cup to Bannon.

"That's mighty nice of you . . . sir," the young rider said, "but the doc's invited us to vittles already."

"Well, my offer's good anytime."

Marshal Rand explained that he had suggested the farm boy should go to the fort and request help. His manner of speaking was much gentler than earlier. McCallister pursed his lips and nodded affirmatively. Bannon took a sip of the coffee, then another, and sat the cup down on the lawman's desk. Rand's displeasure at this wasn't noticed.

"That's good advice, son," Star said, brought his hand to his chin for an instant, then continued, "Say, I've got to go there tomorrow morning anyway. Fort Dodge. I'd sure like the company. Especially if there are Indians about."

Bannon hesitated and then agreed. Letting those savages get away with this horrible nightmare couldn't be allowed. Going to the army was something he must do. The farm boy grinned self-consciously, nodded affirmatively, and introduced himself. As they shook hands, the saloon keeper introduced himself by name and repeated his offer for a free meal.

"Where are you staying tonight, Tyrel?" McCallister asked.

Bannon hesitated, then said, "Well, that's a good question, Mr. McCallister. Haven't been in any place particular for a long time . . . assumin' you don't count the ground. But I reckon we'll be bunkin' in the doctor's stable, if he'll have us."

"Good, why don't I just meet you there in the morning?" McCallister suggested. "At Dr. Tremons's. Say, daybreak?"

"Okay. I appreciate your help, Mr. McCallister."

"Glad you're going along."

Out of curiosity, Marshal Rand asked the saloon keeper what he had to do at the fort. McCallister explained simply that it was business.

Bannon excused himself to leave, grabbed his shotgun, and opened the door. Behind the young rider, Rand's flat voice ordered, "Leave your guns here, Texas. You can get them when you leave Dodge."

Without turning to face the lawman, the young rider paused as if considering the command, then said simply, "I'm leaving tomorrow," and stepped outside. He slammed the door behind him. Expecting the marshal to follow and not watching where he was walking, he stepped into two women coming from the other direction.

Apologizing, he touched the brim of his worn-out hat with his hand. They fluttered and continued their journey. He glanced back at the marshal's unopened door, then hurried to the wagon and jumped aboard, barely touching the front wheel for leverage. His pistol clanged against the seat as he sat, reminding him of the lawman's order and his own defiance. Captain sprang from the wagon's bed and sat with his head on Bannon's lap. Petting the cur, he tried to calm his own nerves.

Star McCallister's horse, a handsome sorrel with a white foreleg, stood at the reining rail, next to Bannon's wagon. Dried sweat crisscrossed its chest and withers. The young rider figured it was a fitting mount for the nattily dressed man. For a brief moment, he wondered where a saloon owner would be riding so hard, but his eyes caught three hard-looking men watching him from across the street. Bannon clucked to his horses and headed back to Dr. Tremons's place.

He reconsidered his decision to go to Fort Dodge tomorrow. Mr. Carlson, the Triple C rancher, would certainly understand that one farm boy, one cook, and a nearly-dead trail boss couldn't do much to get back a herd from a band of Indians no one wanted to find. Of course, the man would understand, the young rider told himself.

Aloud, Bannon spoke through gritted teeth, "But I won't understand." It felt good to say those words. Silently he finished the rest of the decision: "Any way you paint it, I would be running. I would know that I'd up and quit just because it got mean."

A strange feeling wandered through him, gaining momentum as he breathed deeply. Each breath brought more resolve. There would be no more hesitation, no more debating with himself. Tomorrow morning, he would go to the fort as Mr. McCallister suggested. But if the army wasn't interested, he would go look for the herd himself. He had to try. He owed it to Mr. Carlson, to Dan Mitchell, to his Triple C friends—and to himself.

CHAPTER 10

"HEY DOC! DOC Tremons!" John Checker yelled, reining up at the doctor's house. The midafternoon sun was dulled by a war party of gray clouds. His big horse was weary and beginning to show it, after the hard push to town. The ranger figured he had two hours at least before the herd hit the streets.

Not much of Dodge City had seemed familiar to him. Certainly not the buffalo hunters' settlement he remembered. Only two or three buildings even looked like they were around then.

He had forced himself to ride past the location where J. D. McCallister's saloon had been; a three-story hotel occupied the space now. The structural change matched his heartfelt sense that this period of his life was over—for him and his sister. Only a dullness remained.

Disciplining himself to move fast but not foolishly so, he had been tracking the Triple C wagon for less than an hour since entering Dodge, following several intended-to-be-helpful directions. All with no results. Maybe now. But maybe this was no better a suggestion than the rest. No wagon was in sight.

The brittle command from inside the house was gruff, "You'd better walk slow, mister. I want to see your hands. An' you'd damn better be sick."

Walking toward the slightly opened doorway, the former ranger said in a loud voice, "Doc Tremons, I'm with the Triple C. I'm John Checker and I'm looking for my friends. Heard they might be here." No response came from inside the house, but the door opened wider.

Checker thought, another wrong place. It would only take a few minutes more to find out for certain. If they weren't here, he would have to quit looking for his friends and concentrate on recruiting some cowhands.

Inside, the office portion of the home was quiet. The room seemed darker than the day. Dr. Tremons, with a double-barreled shotgun in his hands, limped forward to meet Checker's advance through the door.

Waving the weapon in Checker's direction, the doctor said, "You may be speaking true, Mister John Checker, but I would appreciate your not moving for a minute. Hey, Tug! Tug! Come here, will ya?"

From around the corner, where they were fixing a meal in the kitchen, came the Triple C cook and Dr. Tremons's daughter, Sarah Ann.

"Hot damn and new biscuits, John Checker! You are a sight for my old eyes!" Tug exploded.

Dr. Tremons looked at the red-faced cook, then back at the tall ranger and smiled. Grinning widely, Checker extended his hand to the doctor as Tug limped hurriedly toward him. But the ranger's eyes went from the two men back to the doctor's daughter still standing in the doorway between the office and the kitchen.

The lamplight caught her hair, untied and resting against her shoulders, and painted it rich cinnamon. The same glow danced with the shadows across her face, highlighting her flashing eyes and hiding the freckles on her perky nose. Her smile had its own light and made Checker warm all over.

She wore a light brown apron over a plain blue dress, which was accented with white cuffs and a high collar. Checker couldn't help noticing her proud bosom forcing the cloth to its utmost. He blinked and returned to her eyes, which seemed to sparkle with knowing what he saw. She looked away at her father, then to Tug and back to Checker.

"Hello, John. I'm Sarah Ann Tremons. Tug's been telling me all about you and the other Triple C riders," she said.

"Now that's a worrisome report," Checker responded shyly, removing his hat. He felt dirty and embarrassed at his appearance: unshaven face, trail-worn chaps and sweat-stained shirt. His spurs jingled and he wished he'd taken them off before coming inside. His wild Comanche leather tunic seemed out of place in this home. So did his pistol belt. But he was pulled to this young woman like nothing he'd ever felt before. Nothing. But Tug's hearty handshake disrupted the self-assessment for the moment.

"Tug, it's mighty good to see you," Checker said. "Been trying to catch up with your wagon for the better part of an hour."

"The kid should be back soon. He took the wagon to go find a lawman," the bald-headed, bearded cook said. "Dan Mitchell's alive because of Bannon. Ask the doc here."

"So, Tyrel's not hurt. I'm glad the three of you made it." Checker told Tug that Jackson, Clanahan, Reilman, Tex, and Sonny had also survived.

Turning to Dr. Tremons, Checker asked if he could see the trail boss. Dan Mitchell was sleeping hard, still lying on what served as the doctor's operating table. Dr. Tremons explained he didn't want to move the cowman yet. Pillows had been carefully placed on either side of the uncon-scious man to keep him from rolling off.

"Tomorrow, we'll move him to a bed," the doctor ex-plained. "I didn't want to chance reopening that bullet hole. Or more bleeding by moving him. He's been through enough already. More than enough. Tug's right. The lad saved his life."

Barely breathing, it seemed to the ranger, but the doctor assured him the cattleman was weak but was going to be fine. Checker stared at his friend, without speaking, for long minutes. Sarah Ann walked up and stood beside Checker as he studied his sleeping friend.

For John Checker, the soft ginger scent of Sarah Ann Tremons reinforced her closeness and made it difficult to think at all. All that mattered was having her next to him. How could he be thinking so foolishly at a time like this? About a woman he just met?

"Don't worry, your friend is going to be almost as good as new," she said to Checker. She rested her right hand over his left, where it lay on the table.

Suddenly, Tug came bouncing over, splashing the drink in his hand. Both Checker and the doctor's daughter stepped away from each other. Her hand discreetly moved back to her side.

The trail-drive cook barked, "Hey, Checker, you should taste that stew this here lady an' me been a-puttin' together. It'll make ya fergit ma's cookin'!"

"Have you eaten?" Sarah Ann asked. "Tug and I have been putting some finishing touches on a beef stew. He's quite the cook, as you already know."

"Thank you, ma'am, but I can't stay," Checker replied, noticing Tug's bearded face was more red than usual.

"Call me Sarah Ann," she said.

"Yes, m-m . . . Sarah Ann. Thank you, I wish I could. Tug, where is Tyrel?" Checker's eyes never left her face.

The red-faced cook looked upset. "You just got here! Can't you stay? It's gonna be a slam-bang of a stew. That's not very polite to these here nice folks."

"Hell, yes, Checker! An' how about a little whiskey to whet your appetite?" Dr. Tremons asked, already pouring two glasses half full of the brown liquid.

Checker finally turned away from Sarah Ann and looked at her father. "Well, thanks, Doc. All that sounds mighty good. But we've located our herd an—"

"The herd! Is that what you said? Where'd you find it? Were them Injuns doin' a big heehaw about gettin' all that beef?" Tug gleefully cleared his whiskey with one swallow.

"It's not Indians, Tug. It's rustlers. White men. An'

they're pushing our herd to town now. They're probably two hours away at the most." The ranger's words carried a sense of urgency.

"Young Bannon's coming up the walk right now," Dr. Tremons reported as he glanced through the shutter. He moved to open the door.

"Whose hoss is that out there?" the young rider asked excitedly as he entered with the three-legged dog trailing him. "That's John Checker's big black!"

"And he was riding it," Checker said with a smile as he moved toward the doorway. "How are you, Tyrel?"

Bannon couldn't believe his eyes. His jaw dropped and stayed open. It couldn't be! Dr. Tremons and Tug enjoyed his stunned reaction. Checker gave him a handshake, then a brisk hug.

Checker told Bannon about the other Triple C riders who had made it and about finding the herd. Bannon couldn't hold back the tears when he heard Jackson was alive. He wiped his face with the one sleeve that remained on his shirt. Dr. Tremons then introduced his daughter.

Checker repeated for the pale farm boy what he had told Tug earlier about the stolen herd, that it was rustlers and not Indians, and added that Henry Seals was in on the crime. Bannon was stunned, but the feisty cook choked and sputtered, repeating Seals's name in an involved, drawn-out curse. Immediately, the cook apologized to Sarah Ann and Dr. Tremons.

"Tyrel, we need to ride," Checker said "I'm hoping to get some Texas boys to help meet them coming in. You take the wagon. My black's about done for the day, but I don't want to take the time to switch."

Bannon grinned and blushed. Then he told of his experience with the marshal and his plan to ride to the fort tomorrow. Checker listened until the young rider talked about Star McCallister coming into the lawman's office while he was there. A change came over John Checker's face, like a green meadow getting hit with an unexpected winter storm.

"What was this Star McCallister wearing?" the former ranger asked.

"Oh, a fancy suit. Dude hat. Gray, yeah gray. Kinda dusty, though. His horse had been ridden hard."

"What kind of horse?" Checker asked.

"A fine-lookin' sorrel," Bannon answered.

"With a white foreleg?" Checker asked again.

"Well, yeah, how'd you know?" Bannon asked, confused by the sudden change in the ranger's expression.

The pain of yesterday hit Checker's face full force and distorted it for an instant. His half brother was behind all this! Something ripped at his spirit.

"Sonny described him as the leader of the gang that stole our cattle," Checker answered, trying to regain his focus. He explained how McCallister had apparently seen the wagon hitched to trail horses and had come into the marshall's office to see what the young rider knew. He probably wanted to know where Bannon would be when the herd came in.

"Why ride with me to the fort tomorrow?"

"Great alibi," Checker responded. "Who'd think the gang leader would be helping solve the crime?"

"Well, we'd better get at it then," Bannon said.

"Tug, I'd like you to stay here . . . just in case they come here." Checker nodded toward the cook. "I don't think they'll bother you, Doc, but it never hurts to be ready."

Tug started to say something but thought better of it and kept quiet.

Checker said his goodbyes to Dr. Tremons, Tug, and Sarah Ann. Bannon tipped his floppy hat toward the doctor and his daughter and followed the ranger out the door.

Walking a few steps behind the tall ranger, Tyrel Bannon was intimidated by the elegance of the Long Branch saloon. He glanced down at his trail-worn chaps and one-sleeved shirt. His first impulse was to turn around and leave.

Checker had shoved his gun belt into his saddlebags before they came in. His Colt, however, was shoved into his boot. He suggested Bannon just check his weapon when they got in.

The richly decorated barroom seemed to invite only the wealthiest of cattlemen. It wasn't jammed like most of the other places of entertainment on Front Street. Groups of big-hatted cattlemen smoking black cigars were gathered around tables, drinking and playing cards.

At other tables, cattle buyers in business suits were engaged in the final details of a sale with dust-covered trail bosses. A five-piece orchestra was playing. A billiard table with elaborately carved wooden legs held an active game. There weren't any bar girls soliciting drinks, dances, or other activities.

As he followed Checker, the young rider felt like all eyes were judging him. He swallowed hard to give him enough confidence to keep walking. Once, he almost told Checker that he would wait for him outside with Captain. But at that moment, he bumped into a well-dressed businessman and spilled some of the man's drink on his tailored pants. The farm boy apologized, expecting the worst. The businessman smiled and told him to forget it. Tyrel wondered if Checker was as bothered by all this high-brow activity as he was.

"Wait here, Tyrel," Checker said as they neared the main bar. "This is a step I'd better do alone. I'll be right back. You'll need to check your gun."

"What'll you have?" asked a slick-haired bartender. The young rider awkwardly unbuckled his pistol belt and handed it over.

"Ah, beer. Beer'd be fine," Bannon drawled, watching the busy man wrap his belt around the holstered gun and place it among two dozen others on a nearby shelf. The young rider felt like a part of him had been torn away.

He watched Checker go over to a table where four men were drinking. A full-bearded bear of a man in a white Texas hat was dominating the conversation with a foul string of curses. That was evidently the man Checker sought.

When the bartender served his beer, Bannon asked, "Say, partner, who is that big fellow with the beard . . . over there, by the wall?"

The man looked, still with little interest, and said in a monotone, "That, cowboy, is Shanghai Pierce. They say he's the only man in Texas who can run fifty thousand head on eleven acres of land."

The big cattleman glanced away from his table companions and saw the tall ranger coming. Pierce's face slid from surprised to pleased.

"Well, hello, ranger, how the hell are you? What the hell brings you to Dodge?" the uncouth cattleman bellowed.

"Hello, Shanghai. I need some help."

"Sit down, goddammit. Have a pull," Pierce said without waiting for Checker to respond. "Damn right I'll help ya. Owe ya one, that's for damn certain." He pushed an open chair toward Checker.

"Gentlemen, this here's John Checker, one of the best goddamn lawmen the great state of Texas ever had. Nuthin' like these piss-ant Dodge City starpackers!"

Checker seated himself, nodded to each of the men at the table, and acknowledged Pierce's compliment, "Those are mighty nice words, Shanghai. But I quit rangering. I'm riding for the Triple C."

The big man looked hurt, "Damn, John! If'n ya wanted that, I wish ya'd come to me."

"Would've. But you were long gone by the time I made

up my mind. Got a sister here. Wanted to see her . . . and her family."

"Oh. What can I do fer ya, John?" Pierce brightened.

Checker explained what had happened and that he needed some extra riders to make certain the rustlers didn't try to turn it into another blood bath.

"You got 'em. When do you need 'em?"

"Damn quick. That herd'll be comin' toward the Arkansas later this afternoon. They'll want to move it quick."

"Sure. Sure. Of course they will." Pierce was distracted. He waved his arm to a lanky cowboy across the room. The man came quickly.

"This here's Wade Fuller, my foreman," Pierce told Checker. "Wade, this is John Checker . . . the ranger. Used to be. You've heard me talk about this son of a bitch."

"Yes, sir, honored to shake your hand, ranger."

The big cattleman described the situation in even fewer sentences than Checker had. The foreman asked only where the men should meet him. Checker suggested the north end of the toll bridge. Then he said they should look for his friend and called Tyrel Bannon over.

"Tyrel, this is Shanghai Pierce—and Wade Fuller," Checker said.

"Hello, boy, from what I hear, you can goddamn ride for me any day." Pierce stood, his hand nearly enveloping Bannon's in the handshake. The cattleman gave him a slap on the back that actually stung the farm boy to his toes.

"Thank you, sir. My pleasure."

With a serious frown, Checker said, "Shanghai, I do appreciate your—"

"Hey, spit fire n' damnation, ranger! Coulda been us just as easy as the Triple C. My boys were chompin' at the bit to do somethin' new anyway," Shanghai said, pouring himself a full glass of whiskey. "Hell, if this were goddamn Texas, we'd string all their sorry asses up a tree. Maybe we should.

That goddamn marshal ain't worth a good spit. All he can do is whack Texas cowboys over the head."

Checker shook the big cattleman's hand, then turned to the young rider. "Tyrel, stay with Wade. I'll meet you at the bridge in a few minutes."

"Where're you going?" Bannon asked.

"I'm going to see Star."

"I'll go with you. Star McCallister killed my friends," Bannon snapped, his eyes hard with fury.

They walked together a few steps without Checker responding. He stopped halfway across the big room and turned to the young rider. The men at the table next to them turned to see who it was, then returned to their card playing.

"No, Tyrel. Not this time," Checker said. "This is something I've got to do alone."

"I'm coming with you, whether you say so or not!" Bannon swallowed hard.

Finally Checker spit out what he wanted to say all along, "My father was J. D. McCallister. Star's father. We had different mothers. Star McCallister is my half brother." He glanced around the room, feeling that no one should be listening—or even in the room.

Bannon swallowed and blinked his eyes to keep them from staring. He felt hot and worried about the sudden lack of air.

"Tyrel, there isn't anybody I'd rather have with me in a tight spot than you or Dan Mitchell. An' I'd be saying the same thing if he were here instead of you. But I've got to go see Star—by myself."

With that, Checker walked away. The young rider watched the tall ranger head out the front door of the Long Branch. The young rider could hear the booming voice of Shanghai Pierce behind him.

*　　*　　*

The seven men at the long bar turned to look at John Checker as he entered the Nueces saloon. Star McCallister was nowhere in sight. Four were Texas drovers, and they nodded a greeting that he returned. All four noticed his gun belt, back in place from his saddlebags. The others were locals who watched him without salutation, comment, or motion.

Even in late afternoon, the stale-aired saloon was quieter than most along Front Street. In the far corner, a five-handed poker game was well into high stakes. A gambler with a brushlike mustache was winning. Checker glanced again at the card game as he sat, glimpsing the butt of a pistol under the gambler's black swallowtail coat. He barely heard the short lady with the piled-up hair singing a sad song of love to the rhythm of a grizzled fiddler next to the bar.

Only four other people were in the saloon: a heavy-set businessman eating at a table in the middle of the room, a drunk with faded Confederate pants who had entered a few steps ahead of Checker, a bartender with wiry mutton-chop sideburns, and a buxom waitress.

The businessman, with a gold chain dangling across an expanded vest, avoided eye contact with Checker, pretending to be totally engaged in cutting his steak. The drunk headed straight for the bar and wedged his way between two cowboys.

"Hi, honey, what'll you have?" The bosomy waitress with tired eyes, a thin mouth painted red beyond the lips, and long yellow hair stood beside him, smiling. Her perfume was syrupy; her red, satiny dress featured much cleavage and long, bony legs.

Before he could tell her that he wanted to see Star McCallister, she asked, "Would you like to go upstairs?"

"No thanks, ma'am. Not sleepy. I just need to talk with the boss."

"Sure, sweetie," she responded with a bemused smile. "Herbie—at the bar—he'll show you where Star's at."

She leaned over in front of him to pick up an imaginary speck. Gazing coyly upward, she wanted to make certain the ranger had received an eyeful of her nearly exposed bosom. She was disappointed to see he wasn't looking at her, only studying the room.

"Now, honey, if there's anything else you want . . . you just ask," she said, "My name is Maggie."

"Thanks . . . Maggie."

Checker walked directly to the bartender and said, "I'm looking for Star McCallister."

"So what," the bartender snarled sarcastically.

The tall ranger reached across the bar and grabbed the bartender's shirt, yanking the surprised man off his feet and toward him in one fierce motion. The bartender, now wide-eyed with a face as white as his apron, waved his arms briefly in an awkward struggle but quickly surrendered to the strong grasp below his neck. The room became very quiet.

Checker growled into the man's fearful face, "I've got no time for your games, Herbie. Now—try again."

"Haven't seen him, honest," the bartender pleaded.

"Well, now, Herb, that doesn't quite ring true, does it," came the acid response from the gambler at the poker table.

"Sir, Herbie can advise you that Mister McCallister is in the office . . . in the back. Second door," the gambler continued. "I'll see that and raise you twenty, sir.

He released the pale bartender from his grip. "I'm John Checker," he said to the gambler. "Much obliged."

"Any time. I'll call that."

"When I come back out, Herbie, I'd better see both of your hands," Checker growled, "and they'd better be empty or holding a beer."

Checker tapped lightly on the closed office door,

snapped it open, and stepped inside McCallister's office. The room was small with no windows; a large roll-top desk and chair were the only pieces of furniture. A painting of a naked woman adorned one wall.

The ranger closed the heavy oaken door behind him and faced Star McCallister. It had been years since either had seen the other; the child in both had long since disappeared into manhood. Yet they would have known each other anywhere. Graying light fell across McCallister's emaciated face, making him appear skeletonlike. He sat in the chair, startled from an entry book by Checker's arrival.

Checker seemed to fill the entire door frame. McCallister's eyes fluttered as the image of his own father flickered for an instant in the stern face before him. He quickly recovered from the shock of seeing Checker and hid his emotions behind a smiling facade.

"What can I do for you, sir?" McCallister asked in a most polite voice, laying his pen on the opened pages he was reviewing.

"I need some help, Star," the ranger responded, his voice cracking like a bullwhip in the grayness of the room.

"I'll do what I can," the saloon keeper said, wary but confident. He leaned back in the chair and put both hands behind his head to listen.

"I'm missing some cattle."

"Gosh, I don't understand . . . have you talked with the marsh—"

"No, I came here first," Checker interrupted, "because it was your men that took them. After they murdered my friends."

"What? What are you talking about?" McCallister exclaimed, his eyes were wide, his face drawn. He leaned forward as if in pain, and his hands followed, grasping his stomach. His fingers slid toward the hidden pearl-handled pistol in the shoulder holster.

"Star, don't try it. You aren't that good," the ranger commanded. The words came like Comanche lances. He stepped closer to McCallister, an arm's length away, staring down at his half brother.

The blond saloon keeper's eyes fluttered. He reached out and touched Checker's forearm as a salutation.

"Hello, John. It's been a long time. Have you seen our sister yet?" McCallister grinned like a cougar.

A shiver ran along·Checker's neck and his head. He'd seen smiles like that before. The weight of his Colt against his hip pushed the shiver away.

"A minute ago, you didn't know who I was, Star," Checker barked. "Get up. We're going to meet the herd."

"No."

"No?"

"I know you, John Checker. I know your sister. You wouldn't shoot me." McCallister's voice changed again into a sarcastic snarl, and his thin mouth matched its loathing. "It's not in you, Checker. As much as you hate my guts, you won't kill me. I'm staying right here. Do what you want."

A vicious slap from Checker's open right hand exploded against the side of McCallister's cheek, driving the crooked saloon keeper's jaw sideways and throwing him against the back of his chair. Checker's second slap with his left hand slammed against McCallister's face from the other side. The blow spun the saloon keeper out of his chair and onto the floor.

The small-framed man's mouth filled with blood; his teeth were crimson squares. His whole head was reeling. Tears poised at the corners of his eyes, and McCallister's hands came up in terrified surrender.

"I said we were going. Now!" demanded Checker, his face hot with anger.

The saloon keeper fumbled for words. Putting one hand on the back of the chair, he stood uneasily. Checker yanked the pearl-handled pistol from McCallister's shoulder holster.

"Please . . . please, this is all a mistake, John. I didn't know—"

"What didn't you know? That I would leave the camp to see my sister? That I would be an easy target for three of your men, coming from her house? That sleeping men could be easily butchered? What didn't you know, Star?" Checker's face was purple with rage. "You son of a bitch. You killed innocent men. How many times have you done that? You're worse than your miserable excuse for a father!"

A maniacal laugh burst from McCallister's mouth. His face, crinkled with the just-inflicted wounds, looked more like a jack-o-lantern than a man.

"You never got over that, did you, Checker?" McCallister taunted. "You and your sister are bastards. That's what this is all about."

"No, Star. You're wrong. Again. This is about murder. An' rustling," Checker said so calmly that McCallister was puzzled. "We're going to ride out to the herd. It'll be coming in sight soon. With Henry Seals leading."

The slightly built man, his gray suit now sprinkled with blood, headed for the door but couldn't resist saying, "Where's that naive farm boy friend of yours, Checker? Crying like a baby somewhere . . . or lookin' for soldiers?"

The two men walked out of the office with McCallister in the lead. The saloon keeper alternated between holding his jaw to ease the throbbing and dabbing at his bloody, swelling lips with a handkerchief. They stepped through the narrow hallway, past the bar, and into the main room of the saloon.

Checker noted only the three local people—and the Confederate drunk—remained at the bar; the four cowboys were gone. The drunk was trying to talk one of them into buying him a drink. The bartender watched them out of the corner of his eye as he pretended to wash a glass. The five men at the poker table were engrossed in their game.

The fat businessman belched repeatedly in salute to his just-finished glass of beer. Too late, Checker caught the slight head movement of the buxom waitress toward the shadow-darkened west wall. Three men in long trail coats stood in the shadows with pistols in their hands.

"That's far enough, Checker," spoke the snake-faced man called Waco. One of his ivory-handled Colts was pointed at Checker. The matching gun rested in the killer's shoulder holster.

Beside him was Iron, the square-jawed outlaw, and Ferguson, a nervous man wearing two crossed pistol belts and holding a Colt in each hand. Iron gave a curt warning to Waco. Waco smirked and said something Checker couldn't hear. Iron shook his head affirmatively; a half snear took command of his face and dull eyes. The third man seemed irritated by the interplay, his eyes bouncing from one place in the room to another.

The three men at the bar moved away in haste, walking to the door like someone was pushing them from behind. Only the rebel drunk remained, trying to convince the bartender to give him a drink on the house. The poker game disintegrated, and each player dove, in concert, under the table or behind a nearby chair. Two collided, going for the same place.

The three outlaws separated from each other with several side steps as they advanced, fanning out. Checker stood silent and unmoving. He took a deep breath to push away the nervousness.

"Afternoon, boys. Seen any Triple C beef lately? Or have you been too busy playing Indian," Checker spat. They had expected him to be afraid, getting caught alone. But showing fear wouldn't help him. Inside, he was crawling with bugs. His black-handled Colt only an instinct away.

"So—this is the great John Checker," Waco said, strolling toward McCallister and the ranger, his face bright with the desire to kill. "He don't look so tough to me."

Star McCallister regained his poise and proclaimed loudly to Waco, "Thanks, Mister. This man was trying to rob me . . . take all my money. I don't know what I would have . . ."

Waco chuckled; so did Iron but he wasn't certain why. Ferguson was like a clothesline in the wind, swinging his two guns back and forth in a continuing survey of the room. McCallister turned around and pulled his own pearl-handled pistol from Checker's belt.

"Sorry, brother. Sometimes it goes that way," he said, but Checker's hard face had their father's glare. McCallister winced and hesitated taking the ranger's pistol.

CHAPTER 11

"DROP YOUR GUNS! Move and I'll shoot."

The command was like a rifle shot itself. The heavy cocking of the pistol hammer that followed made it an ominous threat. McCallister froze. So did Iron, his eyes widening like a frightened deer.

Ferguson was startled, dropped the gun in his left hand, and accidently fired the other weapon. Its bullet thudded into the far east wall. Waco swung his head toward the saloon doorway but left his gun pointed at Checker.

Standing there was the young rider. Tyrel Bannon. In his fist was a big Walker Colt. Beside him was a growling three-legged dog. Captain trotted swiftly to face Iron, showing a mouthful of white teeth, and a desire to attack. Iron took a frightened step back, looking first at Bannon, then at Waco for instructions. The young rider did nothing to quiet the dog's grumbling display.

"That's jes' that goddamn farm boy Seals told us about. He ain't nuthin'," Waco assessed without moving. "Take 'im."

"In case you're wonderin'—this farm boy can shoot," Bannon said confidently. "Or didn't Seals tell you that."

He took another step into the room. None of the outlaws dropped their weapons. Only Iron moved, still stutter-stepping backward to keep distance between himself and the ugly cur. He raised his pistol toward Captain.

"Don't try," Bannon said simply.

The dim-witted outlaw dropped the weapon. Its thud sang in the still room. The businessman seemed oblivious to the tension. From under the table, one of the poker players said "Let's get out of here!" Another said, "Wait. I want to see this." Maggie, the waitress, was slowly easing her way to the back door, her back against the far wall, her breasts heaving with fear.

"These old Walkers are something, aren't they?" the young rider continued. "Ever see the hole they put in a man?"

He took another step, his Colt moving evenly from one outlaw to the next to the next.

" 'Course you might want to take a chance. Seals said I was just a farm boy. Let's see . . . three, no, four against . . . two. You know, this here Walker might misfire, too. Done that a few times."

He spread his feet, facing Waco and Ferguson. The latter was sweating heavily, his eyes alternating between the gun in his hand, the one on the floor, and the young rider in front of him.

"Better figure, though, on two of you not makin' it," Bannon continued. "That's not counting what my ranger friend will do."

Checker couldn't help grinning. Appearing to enjoy the encounter, the young rider's own mouth curled upward.

"Almost forgot. That's not the worst of it, boys," Bannon said. "Outside are twenty Texas cowboys . . . itchin' to string you up. Texans don't like rustlers . . . an' we hate murderers.

"There's only one thing standing between you and the rope. The ranger here. He won't let 'em do it. So if you shoot us two . . . well, you get the picture. Now that there is the longest speech I ever made. But I'm through talking. Drop your guns or open the ball."

Star McCallister's shoulders sagged. He caught Checker's eyes, then looked beyond them and let the pistol fall from his opened hand. Waco turned his hand and opened his fist to let the pistol lay in his flat palm, then let it slide from his fingers to the floor. Ferguson apologized for firing his gun, babbling about not being hanged. He took a step toward the young rider, bent his knees, and laid his second pistol carefully next to the first weapon on the saloon floor.

Bright-eyed, Bannon asked the ranger what he wanted to do with the four unarmed men. Bannon called for Captain to come back to his side, and the young rider crouched to greet the returning dog. At that moment of distraction, Waco reached for the untouched gun in his shoulder holster.

No one saw the ranger draw. Checker's first shot drilled Waco inches above the belt buckle. The second shot to the outlaw's midsection followed so quickly that the two cracks sounded like one long explosion. The punch of both bullets threw the snake-faced man against the pompous businessman seated at his table, catching him with a mouthful of potatoes.

Both Waco and the fat man were instantly flopping together on the floor like two bobcats fighting. Breaking free, the businessman vomited as he knelt on all fours. The snake-faced outlaw screamed with gut-shot pain. His hands were bright red as he tried to hold his stomach together where a red circle was blossoming.

"Help me, Star! I-I-I'm gut shot!" Waco's groan was throaty and wild.

"Shut up, you stupid bastard!" McCallister blurted. His eyes fluttered, and his body shivered as if the eyelids totally controlled him.

Checker replaced the two empty shells with new loads, spun the cylinder, and reholstered the Colt. Through the doors thundered eight of Shanghai Pierce's men, each with a Winchester.

"What's going on here?" the first one hollered, his store-bought hat pushed back on his head.

"Everything's under control, boys," Checker said, "thanks to my young friend here."

Muscling his way through the crowd of cowboys and gathering onlookers came Marshal Jubal Rand. Unnecessarily, he shoved the last two trail riders out of the way and demanded to know what was happening.

"Hello, Marshal. I'm John Checker, formerly of the Texas Rangers," Checker said.

"You rangers ain't got no authority here," Rand replied.

"No argument there, Marshal. Just wanted you to know which side we were coming from."

McCallister blurted, "Jubal, these two men tried to rob me! This . . . this man on the floor . . . was shot . . . trying to stop them. Isn't that right, Herb? Arrest them, Marshal. They're everything we don't need in Dodge."

Marshal Rand responded immediately to the suggestion and said briskly, "It's against the law to carry a gun in town. I'm arresting all of you for violating the ordinance. My deputies are coming behind me—with shotguns. We'll see about the other matter when you're behind bars."

McCallister smiled and bent over to retrieve his pistol. Checker stepped on his hand and held it down.

"No, Marshal. Not this time." Checker's words were like a fist to the stomach, "We've lost a lot of friends to this man—and his gang. An' we've had our herd taken. We can't bring our friends back—but we can get our cattle. An' we're going to do just that."

Marshal Rand had the drop on the ranger, whose arms were folded in front of him. Yet Rand was uneasy about the situation. There was something about John Checker that made a man worry when the words got hard. No matter what the appearances were. Rand hadn't lived this long without paying attention to little signals, ones that men who didn't live by the gun never saw—until it was too late. He glanced at Star's hand under Checker's boot.

Checker pointed with his left hand in the direction of the three outlaws, letting his right hand drop to his gun belt. His thumb rested on top of the belt buckle and held his gun hand in place, a fraction of a second away from the black-handled Colt with the white elk-bone circles. "These two men—and the bloody one on the floor—should be arrested for murder."

"You got any proof of that?" Rand asked.

"My word," the former ranger answered.

"I saw it," came the wobbly voice of Maggie, the waitress, still pushed against the wall. "They were going to shoot him."

"I'll back that up, too," came the gambler's icy reinforcement.

From the floor where he knelt, the fat businessman tried to sound important and said, "There is no question that these three hooligans were seeking to murder this fine . . . ranger."

At the bar, the Confederate drunk poured himself a drink from the bottle sitting there, raised his filled glass in triumph, and garbled, "Long live Robert E. Lee!"

Pulled in that direction by the salutation, Checker looked at the green-faced bartender trying to make up his mind about what to say. The ranger advised, "Herbie, right now you're just a bystander. A lie makes you one of them."

The bartender shook his head up and down six times as fast as he could to affirm his understanding. He untied his apron, laid it on the bar, and walked toward the entrance. Cowboys and onlookers let him pass.

Marshal Jubal Rand looked like someone had hit him in the face with a bucket of water. He took a deep breath, then another. Behind him, more of Shanghai Pierce's men entered the saloon. Each was somber and each carried a Winchester; most wore handguns as well. One handlebar-mustached cowboy greeted Checker warmly. The ranger responded in kind. McCallister pulled on his hand and Checker put more weight on it. Tears of pain were trickling down the crooked saloon keeper's cheeks.

"Now see here ranger. I've done business with Star

McCallister." Marshal Rand straightened his back as he spoke. "He runs a fine establishment. You've got the wrong man."

Rand's face reddened as he spoke; his mouth, a thin line of frustration at being challenged. The young rider wondered why the lawman hadn't asked him about what happened. Occasionally, Bannon's eyes wandered to Waco's agony-twisted body on the floor. Each time he recoiled from the sight.

"Rand, you didn't want to help us earlier." Checker's eyes tore into the marshal's face. "Now, I'm giving you another chance to act like a lawman. Put these two in jail and go with us to get our herd back. Star McCallister is their leader, so I'm taking him with us. After we get the herd, he'll stand trial for murder and rustling when we return."

The former ranger paused, looked down at the boot holding his half-brother's hand in place, and returned his gaze to the lawman, without removing his foot.

"Make no mistake about it, Rand. There will be justice today. With you or without you. It doesn't matter to me. But I'll bet it does to your city council." Checker's words made Rand swallow. "If that's not clear enough, call off your deputies or the town will be looking for a new marshal."

McCallister started to say something, but the increased pressure from Checker's boot convinced him otherwise.

Marshal Jubal Rand ran his tongue along his upper lip and said, "Ranger, I ride with you. My deputies will put these two in jail. They'll stand trial for murder."

On the far side of the river, Henry Seals swelled with pride as he sat in the saddle, watching the Triple C herd move in a huge circle onto flat grazing land with the river cutting off their advance on the north and a soft ridge keeping them in place on the south. Steers were stretched all the way over the ridge and beyond. McCallister men were working them smoothly forward.

For reassurance, Seals patted his shirt one more time to feel the trail papers stuffed inside. To his back was Dodge City; he could almost taste drink and women. McCallister had told him to leave immediately after the sale, but the turncoat cowboy had decided to give himself a proper celebration first. He had earned it.

Seals glanced down at his shirt again, this time to make certain it was tucked properly into his pants. His entry should be one befitting a trail boss. As planned, he would go alone to the Long Branch saloon, where most of the cattlemen—and buyers—congregated to make their deals. He hadn't been in the famous place before. It wasn't a regular cowboy's bar. It was more dignified, more elegant, more expensive. Just the idea of walking into the Long Branch titillated Seals.

Satisfied, he looked over at the Arkansas River bridge into town. At the north entrance, where there had been nothing a moment before, came twenty-four riders. Probably some cowboys from another drive fascinated by the size of the herd and wanting a closer look. The renegade Triple C drover straightened his back and drew in a breath to pull up his chest.

Suddenly he realized Star McCallister was with them. What was he doing? He had said to meet him in the Nueces. Then he recognized the horseman beside him. John Checker! Damn! He knew something would happen when two of the three outlaws sent to kill Checker caught up with the herd and announced they hadn't succeeded.

Tyrel Bannon! Astride that brown horse of Sonny Jones's. What the hell is this? Where was Waco? Iron? Ferguson? Sunlight reflected from something metallic on another rider's shirt. A lawman? Seals swiveled in the saddle toward the working riders and called out. But the noise of the cattle was too much for him to be heard.

His hand stretched toward the butt of his Winchester resting in the saddle boot. One realization stopped him: if he drew the gun, he would die. Here on this ground, next to the Arkansas river. Here he would breathe his last. His blood would seek the Kansas dirt and no one would care.

He remembered John Checker's stare when the beaten Seals reached for his pistol after his fist fight with Bannon. The image followed of Sonny Jones challenging him moments before Checker spun around. Both triggered the memory of the aches he carried long after the farm boy finished pummeling him. No. He was a cowhand, not a gunman. Nobody was paying him enough to face John Checker—or even the farm boy. Henry Seals gulped his remaining nerve and sat his horse, watching the riders advance.

The rest of the McCallister men worked the herd, paying little attention to the group from town headed toward them. They were surprised to see other cowboys coming but figured it was the way the buyer wanted it. Anyway, the sooner someone else had the herd, the sooner they could celebrate like Star had promised.

As Star McCallister, John Checker, Tyrel Bannon, and Marshal Rand advanced, the riders behind them spread out and began to flank the herd. Without appearing to do so, each cowboy rode alongside a different McCallister gang member, positioning himself to put the man under his direct fire.

Checker and McCallister cantered in front of the paralyzed Seals. Alongside them was Marshal Jubal Rand; his badge shone like a hole of light was on his shirt.

"Give me the papers, Seals," the ranger demanded and held out his hand.

Seals looked first at McCallister and winced. The saloon keeper's face was battered, his lower lips already swelling, his eyes reddened and lowered. Seals saw the gang leader's right hand was purple and swollen. Hurriedly, Seals popped a button from his shirt to get the documents.

He handed them to Checker and said, "I-I-I didn't have any choice, Checker . . . honest. I w-w-wanted . . ."

"Save it, Seals," snapped McCallister without looking up.

"A rope's too good for you, Seals. Why don't you reach for that six-gun in your belt. Give me a reason," Checker said, his eyes ripping the cowboy's face apart.

From over the far ridge came four more riders waving joyously: Sonny Jones, Randy Reilman, Tex, and Jackson. Checker and Bannon waved back.

Jackson slid into place alongside a Norwegian man with an immense belly. His shirt buttons had given up on their task of covering an extended stomach, leaving a wide sliver of long johns showing. Discolored suspenders were almost to the same point of surrender. Jackson smiled a welcome, and the Norwegian responded with a silly grin of his own.

Tex picked out another rustler to watch. The handsome cowboy's broken leg swung free of his stirrup; two straight sticks held it straight, laced tightly in place with long strips of cloth. The head-bandaged wrangler, Randy Reilman, wheeled up alongside Tex and rattled off a series of curses at the outlaw that made his friend laugh.

Sonny Jones searching for trouble he hoped to find, recognized a man riding for McCallister and rode up alongside him. The broad-shouldered rustler asked if Sonny was there to join them. Sonny shook his head and said, "I quit that, Tom. You're ridin' on the wrong side. That's John Checker over there."

The rustler spun his head around to look, then returned his gaze to Sonny, who said, "You killed my friends, Tom. If it was mine to do, I'd shoot you down where you stand."

Tyrel Bannon and the three-legged dog rode up to a short cowboy with a long scar angled across his right cheek up to his forehead and over his eyelid. The young rider touched his hand to his hat in a greeting. The McCallister man frowned, spat a long stream of tobacco toward the cur, and looked away. Captain's back hunched and a low growl forced the man to keep checking the dog's distance.

Slowly, like a creek filling from a spring rain, the McCallister gang realized something was very wrong. Checker,

Seals, and the saloon keeper continued riding to the closest rustlers. The other outlaws turned to fully comprehend what was behind them. Each saw a Winchester or two leveled at his stomach.

Checker drew his Colt and announced, "Men, you are surrounded by good Texas cowboys. They'd love to put you six feet under. Even if the gunfire does start the herd running. Unbuckle your iron—or I tell them to open up."

Seals breathed in deeply, loosened his pistol belt, and let it fall. His agitation obvious, he spoke to the men who appeared to be undecided about their next move. "Men, do what he says. Don't shoot. Don't do anything! Please!"

None of the rustlers moved, but none seemed inclined to start anything. Each man seemed to be waiting for the other to unbuckle his gun—or go for it. They stared at Star McCallister, whose eyes would not meet theirs.

"This is our herd!" growled one outlaw in a high-crowned hat, a bandolier of rifle bullets over his shoulder. As he spoke, the outlaw grabbed for the pistol stuck in his belt.

Checker fired, hitting him in the shoulder and spinning the man to the ground. A crimson blotch spread across his brown shirt. He curled up like a baby, grabbing his broken shoulder; his face was tortured with pain.

Long-horned heads rose and searched for trouble. Steers all the way to the ridge were suddenly alert. But no other shots came. While some acted like they wanted an excuse to run, the rest of the trail-savvy herd seemed content enough to wait. Grazing gradually took over any fear.

"Anyone else?" Checker shouted. "Come on! Do it! I'll chase this herd to hell if I have to. You bastards killed our friends. Come on, somebody—"

From the far end of the herd, Jackson yelled out, "Now, Checker, don't you have all the fun. Leave some for us. In case it isn't perfectly clear, boys, you have an immediate choice. Lose your hardware . . . or lose your lives."

All heads whipped to the direction of the new voice.

At the other end came a second voice. Sonny's. Full and strong. "You heard them. But I'd prefer you'd pull leather," he said, his eyes judging each man for courage or foolishness.

"What is this? We're just cowhands bringing a herd to town. Are you stealing from us . . . in broad daylight?" a huge cowboy said in a voice so high-pitched and thin that it didn't sound right.

"Tell them, McCallister, I'm getting impatient," Checker said.

"He's got the papers, Wes. It's over. Do what he says, you stupid idiot."

Captain's teeth bristled and a fierce growl came from his belly. The short man beside Bannon shivered and slowly pulled his handgun from its holster and let it drop beside his horse's hooves. The surprised animal danced sideways and the cowboy mouthed, "I'm sorry."

The young rider sensed Checker's readiness. And Sonny's. He could feel Jackson's tension without seeing his friend directly. Inside, Tyrel Bannon himself was cold. Inside he wanted them to go for their guns. It was a feeling of revenge he had never known. He didn't like it but it was there.

Six more pistols hit the soft earth. Followed by three Winchesters, then three more revolvers. It was over. Bannon sought Checker's eyes for approval, then Jackson's. He thought there was a slight disappointment on the ranger's face but it might have been only the shadow from his hat.

Marshal Rand took the opportunity to assert his authority with a ringing statement. "You men are under arrest for murder and cattle rustling . . . by the authority invested in me by the state of Kansas"—he paused, glanced at Checker, and continued—"and the state of Texas." Checker nodded his approval.

The marshal ordered the outlaws to dismount and leave

their horses behind with the herd. Shanghai's men stayed with the cattle as planned. Soon the disarmed McCallister men crossed the bridge and shuffled onto the street toward the city jail. Four deputies waited outside.

Star McCallister walked last in line, his face disturbed and grim. A few steps in front of him was a subdued Henry Seals. Jackson, Tyrel Bannon, John Checker, Sonny Jones, Randy Reilman, and Tex came behind them, like a town parade.

Jackson was reciting Shakespeare to the beaming young rider; Checker was talking with Sonny about liking Dodge City. Tex and Reilman were watching the marshal posture authoritatively for the onlookers. Captain ran in and out of the horses, yipping excitedly.

Suddenly, Star McCallister stopped. His thin face distorted like a blanket pulled from opposite sides by fighting children. He screamed shrilly, "This is all my father's fault! I wish he'd never met that whore who spawned you and your sister! She's nothing an' neither are you. Why did you even come back?!"

"Shut up, McCallister, or we'll hang you now," Reilman snapped. "You killed our friends; we don't even know your goddamn family!"

"Yeah, nobody here is your brother or your sister, McCallister," growled Tex. "Ain't no coyotes around to claim you either."

"Maybe your pappy shoulda taught you not to steal goddamn Texas beef," added a red-faced Reilman.

"Hell, maybe he was as crazy as you," Tex laughed and the others joined in.

Only the young farm boy and the former ranger knew what McCallister was talking about. The others figured he had cracked under the pressure of arrest. Bannon wanted to say something to Checker but knew it wasn't necessary.

As if he hadn't heard the distraught McCallister, Checker slapped Sonny on the back as they rode and told

him where Tug was and that Dan Mitchell was alive. Tex
and Reilman shouted to McCallister to shut up and keep
moving. Almost at the same time, both said something
about the man losing his mind.

From around the corner came a buggy driven by Dr.
Tremons. Sarah Ann was with him, her arm around a pale
but conscious Dan Mitchell wrapped in a blanket. On a
gray, dancing horse was Tug, grinning from ear to ear and
holding his shotgun.

The testy doctor yelled first, "This tough ol' bird woke
up an' wouldn't leave us alone—until we brought him here
to see how you were!"

Dan Mitchell smiled; the weakness of it belied his feeling. "Hello, boys. I see we've got our herd back. Thanks."

"Goldurn it! I missed all the fun!" Tug hollered, waving
the prized weapon.

The Triple C riders rode over to the buggy, each eager
to greet their trail boss. The first was the young rider. Dan
Mitchell reached forward with his right hand to shake
Bannon's.

"Thanks, cowboy. You're drawing top-hand wages."

Sarah Ann's eyes sought the ranger's and found them.
Sonny looked first at her, then at Checker, and grinned.

"Looks to me like the ranger's found time to do some
courting in between chasing down our beeves," the happy
cowboy laughed. Tyrel Bannon turned in his saddle
toward John Checker and chuckled.

Sarah Ann blushed, lowered her eyes for an instant,
then brought them up again. Checker's eyes were waiting.

The former ranger looked around and proclaimed,
"After we sell this herd, everybody's coming out to my sister's place . . . to celebrate."

THE GALLOWSMAN

WILL CADE

Ben Woolard is a man ready to start over. The life he's leaving behind is filled with ghosts and pain. He lost his wife and children, and his career as a Union spy during the war still doesn't sit quite right with him, even if the man sent to the gallows by his testimony was a murderer. But now Ben's finally sobered up, moved west to Colorado, and put the past behind him. But sometimes the past just won't stay buried. And, as Ben learns when folks start telling him that the man he saw hanged is alive and in town—sometimes those ghosts come back.

___4452-8 $4.50 US/$5.50 CAN

Dorchester Publishing Co., Inc.
P.O. Box 6640
Wayne, PA 19087-8640

Please add $1.75 for shipping and handling for the first book and $.50 for each book thereafter. NY, NYC, and PA residents, please add appropriate sales tax. No cash, stamps, or C.O.D.s. All orders shipped within 6 weeks via postal service book rate. Canadian orders require $2.00 extra postage and must be paid in U.S. dollars through a U.S. banking facility.

Name_____
Address_____
City_____ State_____ Zip_____
I have enclosed $_____ in payment for the checked book(s).
Payment <u>must</u> accompany all orders. ❑ Please send a free catalog.

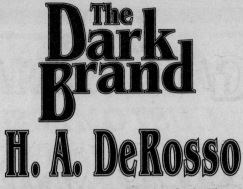

The Dark Brand

H. A. DeRosso

Driscoll made a mistake and he's paying for it. They stuck him in a cell—with a man condemned to hang the next morning. Driscoll learns how his cellmate robbed a bank and killed a man...and how the money was never recovered. But he never learns where the money is. After Driscoll serves his time and drifts back into town, he learns that the loot is still hidden, and that just about everyone thinks the condemned man told Driscoll where it is buried before he died. Suddenly it seems everybody wants that money—enough to kill for it.

___4412-9 $4.50 US/$5.50 CAN

Dorchester Publishing Co., Inc.
P.O. Box 6640
Wayne, PA 19087-8640

Please add $1.75 for shipping and handling for the first book and $.50 for each book thereafter. NY, NYC, and PA residents, please add appropriate sales tax. No cash, stamps, or C.O.D.s. All orders shipped within 6 weeks via postal service book rate. Canadian orders require $2.00 extra postage and must be paid in U.S. dollars through a U.S. banking facility.

Name_____

Address_____

City_____State_____Zip_____

I have enclosed $_____ in payment for the checked book(s).

Payment <u>must</u> accompany all orders. ❑ Please send a free catalog.

CHECK OUT OUR WEBSITE! www.dorchesterpub.com